ASYLUM

Anthony Masters

Constable • London

First published in Great Britain 2003
by Constable, an imprint of Constable & Robinson Ltd
3 The Lanchesters, 162 Fulham Palace Road
London W6 9ER
www.constablerobinson.com

ISBN 1-84119-602-9

Printed and bound in Great Britain

A CIP catalogue record for this book
is available from the British Library

Asylum

Also by Anthony Masters

To Robert, Terri, Luke and Lydia Arnold
With much love

Chapter One

Heavy snow continued to fall. As Rila looked out of her window at the Grand Hotel in the late afternoon the bleakness of a British seaside town in winter seemed temporarily softened. Even the slow-moving traffic was quieter, while pedestrians, aware of the black ice lurking under the snow, picked their way carefully.

Inside, the faded grandeur of the old hotel was sinking into squalor, the partitioned rooms offering the minimum living space. The wallpaper was stained and peeling while plaster continuously fell from the ceilings. Like the snow, thought Rila, as she shivered over the small heater that dried the air but provided only tepid warmth in one corner of the room.

Prowling about, caged by the damp walls, she returned to the window, checking the watch that was the most treasured of the few possessions Rila had managed to bring with her from Kosovo.

She and Stefan had been in England for some months now, spending most of their time in holding centres until they had arrived in Seagate to wait for their papers in what a social worker had described as 'a fresh-air environment'.

A woman on the checkout at the Asda supermarket had told Rila that the town had once been elegant, a bathing place of English nobility, visited by royalty, with spacious Georgian buildings and a promenade bedecked with flags and bunting. But Seagate's days of glory had been over for decades. The elegance had faded, and only a few

Londoners still came for day trips, eating in fish bars, gazing at the closed-down amusement park with the battered sign still advertising Dream World, walking or staggering drunkenly down the promenade, with a few braver souls swimming in the grey, cold waters of the English Channel.

'A fresh-air environment.' The social worker's bright and breezy phrase hammered painfully in Rila's head.

She was waiting for Stefan as she always did, gazing down at Audley Square, waiting for her beloved son to emerge from his primary school a few streets away, running into the square, rucksack on his back, pushing the long black hair out of his eyes.

The Grand Hotel occupied one corner of the square. Opposite was the Asda supermarket, with apartments above as run-down as the Grand, where more asylum seekers waited in limbo. Rila knew they were all spending their days like caged animals, pacing their prisons – prisons that included the snow-bound streets, for she considered Seagate itself to be one enormous cage, hemmed in between the railway line and the sea.

Stefan had only recently started going to school. For months Rila had been too afraid to let him out of her sight. As a result, mother and son had trekked streets lined with boarded-up shops, strangers in a strange land. Were all British towns like this? she wondered. At home she had imagined England as the green and pleasant land depicted in the old editions of the *National Geographic* magazines that Nev, her husband, had treasured. Pastoral cricket on the green, riding to hounds, quaffing ale in thatched pubs, a brook trickling through a meadow, knee-deep in wild flowers, competing marrows at the flower show, the flood-lit village church in white Christmas fields – everything and everywhere glowing with promise.

False promise. Dream World said it all. Seagate was a crumbling, disaffected, disappointing, alarming slum of a town.

As Rila gazed out at the all too familiar view, she took in

the other sides of the square, occupied by the stained concrete of the multi-storey car park that smelt of urine, and the old-fashioned department store, Perkins, that had closed down years ago and was now a cheap furniture warehouse. The name Perkins, faded from wind and rain, still hung over the entrance. On the corner was the HSBC bank and next to that a fish and chip shop that smelt of rancid fat.

But soon Stefan would be running home from school, clattering up the five floors, charging in, wanting his tea, pushing the long black hair out of his eyes yet again and turning her monochrome world into Technicolor.

Rila still blocked out the memories of home. The burning house, the dead that had included husband, mother and two elder sons. The next-door neighbours, familiar for so long, suddenly enemies, attacking, shooting and pillaging, while she and Stefan cowered in the cellar.

They had been rescued by some people who had recently moved in across the street and, somehow, the dead had been buried, except that Rila didn't think they were dead for her loved ones were as alive to her today as they had been the night of the massacre.

Rila was still in shock, traumatized, still mercifully numb, and she clung to Stefan for life and light.

Eventually Rila had been persuaded to allow Stefan to attend school, partly because she knew he wanted to go and partly because of her guilt when the social worker explained patiently, 'You're holding him back, you see.'

Painfully aware of her isolation, Rila wavered. She was terrified of letting Stefan go, but the social worker had made her feel ashamed.

Eventually she allowed herself to be advised by the other Kosovan women in the Grand. The children had to go to school, they insisted. They had to learn the language. They had to belong. When they received a residential permit, all would be well. Wouldn't it?

Rila still hoped England *was* a green and pleasant land, somewhere outside Seagate. For now, while she was seeking asylum under British law, she would have to remain at the Grand and spend her days walking around the town, or, when the weather was too bad, stand staring out of her window. She watched Stefan go to school. She watched Stefan come home again. The rest of the day was a desert and now Rila was watching again, her eyes on the square. Stefan would soon be rounding that corner. Stefan would soon be waving and Rila's heart would feel like bursting with sudden happiness.

'I don't think,' said Fitim Kadric to Edina Milstein, 'that Lorta's visit is a good idea.'

'We should feel honoured,' Mile Kropitz cut in.

'He is not just coming to Seagate. The tour is extensive,' said Josif Genzo. 'It's no more than a piece of icing on the wedding cake. Something cosmetic to seal the knot.'

They were sitting in a sweaty little café by the railway station that all four members of the council saw as neutral ground. Phil's, as the café was known, smelt of vinegar and stewed tea, with the windows steamed up, the fug sharp and clinging.

'Lorta is nothing,' said Genzo. 'He can do nothing.'

'I'm not so sure,' said Edina. 'He's going to be a puppet, isn't he? With the US government pulling the strings.'

'I agree,' replied Fitim Kadric. 'And don't forget Blair is in Bush's pocket. So the UK's in on it as well.'

'They say he could be a peacemaker,' said Edina thoughtfully. 'But in my country there can be no peace. Not in the long term.'

Mile Kropitz was dismayed. 'So what are you saying?'

'We are saying,' put in Fitim Kadric, 'that Lorta will make things worse.'

Boyd and Patterson sat shivering in the van, pulling on their balaclava masks. Then Boyd glanced down at his watch.

'What's the time now?' asked Patterson.

'Coming up to three.'

'God, how I hate this waiting.'

'We've been well rehearsed,' said Boyd. 'Nothing's going to go wrong.'

'Don't give me shit,' muttered Patterson.

The armour-plated security truck slowly edged into Audley Square. The snow was still falling and the wind-screen washer was frozen. As a result, Callaghan decided to pull over and wipe off the snow-bound grime with an oily rag. When he got back inside he saw the result was worse than before.

'Let's go.' Brandon was uneasy.

'We're early.'

'We don't want to get stuck. The forecast's terrible.'

'We should stick to the schedule.'

'We're only a couple of minutes out,' Callaghan assured him.

Stefan was late. He'd been kept behind several times before, and when Rila had gone over to the school to collect him, she'd been told by his teacher, Mrs Grove, that Stefan had been 'cheeky'. He had to be 'in detention'. Rila hadn't understood the first word, but the phrase 'in detention' was all too familiar.

Back home her son had always been top of his class, and even here, despite his lack of English, the Head had told her, 'Stefan is a bright child.'

She suspected the reason Stefan had been kept in was that he'd been bored in class. Mrs Grove had not impressed her.

'Now!' said Boyd and accelerated, sending the van swerving, wrestling with the wheel.

'For Christ's sake –' Patterson was thrown forward and hurriedly did up his seat belt. 'Haven't you noticed the weather?'

'It's snowing,' said Boyd, revving the engine as they entered the square. 'Shit. They're early.'

'They'll be delivering any minute now.' Patterson had lost what little nerve he had, gazing through the snowflakes on the scummy windscreen, seeing one of the security men leap out. Then his colleague joined him. Both were carrying heavy bags and wore helmets and had truncheons at the waist.

The van came to a squealing halt, and within moments Boyd and Patterson were out, wading through deep snow, making as much noise as possible, waving their automatics.

Obedient to the letter of the safety manual Callaghan's and Brandon's hands shot up – dropping the bags which Boyd and Patterson fumbled to pick up from the freezing snow.

'Get down on the ground!' yelled Patterson. Brandon and Callaghan obeyed him without the slightest hesitation.

Passers-by were turning round, pointing, as if they were intent on a piece of street theatre, utterly detached.

A small, almost appreciative crowd was gathering, and for a wild moment Boyd wondered if he should take a hat round at the end of the performance. But he didn't have a hat, only a balaclava, well pulled down over his face.

As Boyd grabbed at one of the bags he saw that a man with staring eyes had just stepped out of the crowd. He held a football raised aloft in his right hand. 'Forty-forty,' he shouted. 'Forty-forty.'

'Fuck off!' yelled Boyd as the man took a few robot-like steps towards him.

Still holding on to the bags, Patterson and Boyd stumbled back to the van and slammed the doors.

'That's all we needed – the local nutter,' complained

12

Patterson as Boyd's hand went to the ignition. But there were no keys.

'Where are they?'

'What?'

'The fucking keys.' Boyd saw them on the floor. How the hell had they slipped out? He snatched them up, rammed one into the ignition. The engine roared and Boyd began to skid the van round in a wide arc. The slush splattered the already filthy windscreen as the wipers churned in their losing battle against the still falling snow.

Rila saw Stefan waving to her from the opposite pavement and she waved back, opening the rusted window with considerable force and watching him begin to run across the square.

Then the fear came, biting deep.

Stefan was running.

A green van was turning, brakes screaming.

The security guards were getting up from the grey snow and running back towards the security truck.

The green van continued to turn, snow flurrying.

Stefan was still running.

The van still turning.

'The boy!' yelled Patterson. 'Watch out for the fucking boy.'

But Boyd could see nothing through the blurred screen. Then he felt the impact and could just make out a dark shape somersaulting backwards, a rucksack spilling school books.

'He's fucking lying there.'

'We can't stop,' said Boyd, trying to turn the van again. Then he felt a bump.

'Now you've run over him,' yelled Patterson. 'You've fucking run over that kid!'

Boyd drove on, trying not to believe what he was hearing. Patterson was a prick. He made too many mistakes. But then Boyd began to realize with a deadening certainty that this was one mistake Patterson hadn't made.

Locked in their driving cabin, Callaghan and Brandon saw the van hit the boy and then reverse off him.

'Christ!' Callaghan kept saying over and over again, while Brandon stared numbly out of the filthy windscreen. 'Oh, my Christ!'

'They've squashed him,' said Brandon. 'They've gone and fucking squashed the kid.'

Rila saw Stefan's rucksack bursting open, scattering books and his lunch-box, and then disappearing under the wheels of the green van.

People were shouting. The van was being driven erratically down the street. Rila could see Stefan lying on the road. He was the wrong shape and there was a dark stain in the snow.

Rila began to scream – a primeval scream that seemed not to be coming from her at all. The sound continued while she threw open the door of the room, remembering the lift was permanently out of order and plunging down the staircase, the foyer like a deep black lake five floors below her. For a moment she wanted to jump and then found herself in the arms of Josep, a widower who lived on the floor below.

'What are you doing?'

'Stefan!' She slapped at him until Josep let her go.

Rila slipped and fell in the impacted snow as she stumbled down the marble steps of the Grand, but she picked herself up as if nothing had happened, running, still screaming to the crowd that was gathering just outside the supermarket.

'Forty-forty,' said the man with staring eyes, football raised high. 'Forty-forty.'

Pushing her way through, the scream now a raucous cry, Rila flung herself down, head pounding, vision glazed, seeing the square as a white-out, scrabbling at the shoulders of someone who was kneeling, his pinstripe suit smeared with dirt.

'Stefan –'

'I'm a doctor. I'm afraid there's nothing I can do.'

'Some doctor,' she yelled at him in English. 'Some fucking doctor.'

He moved aside and for the first time she saw Stefan. The blood was bubbling out of his mouth and below the waistline all she could see was blood-smeared pulp. Stefan's eyes were wide open and there was a half-smile of happy expectation still on his face.

Rila buried her head on her son's chest, listening, although she could hear nothing but the nervous chatter of the crowd.

'Forty-forty,' said the nutter.

Someone pulled her away, but she fought back, kicking and swearing.

Then Rila tried to gather Stefan up in her arms, but slipped and fell again, rolling over, taking him with her, until his shattered body was lying on hers and his blood began to spread across her bosom.

'Forty-forty,' said her tormentor.

Someone told the young man with the football to go away.

Chapter Two

Boyd sat, weeping. The hotel was five miles down the coast in a smarter and more genteel town called East-gate.

Patterson had gone and Creighton sat on the hotel bed, saying nothing, watching Boyd as he sat and cried in the chair by the imitation walnut desk.

'There's nothing, absolutely nothing you could have done,' Creighton said bleakly. 'What happened was an accident. When your wife and children were killed, Danny, you never grieved for them. You won't grieve for this boy either. I've seen you in operation. You bury stuff. Maybe that's why you're good.'

'I need space.'

'I can't spare you.'

'I killed him.'

'It was an accident.'

'I can't handle this.'

'You'll have to.' Creighton was intractable, running true to form.

'You got me to do a robbery. What else do you want me to do? Shoot kids in a classroom –'

'Shut up!'

There was a deep silence in the overheated room. Out-side the snow had stopped and the night was gleaming with frost.

'I need to brief you. In view of what's happened, if I could find someone else for this job I would. But we've started. You're established. So you have to go on. Patterson won't be with you. You'll never see him again. You're on your own.'

Boyd looked up at Creighton for the first time. Their eyes met, and Creighton was the first to look away.

'You know the situation.'

'It's a God-awful place, that rotting town by the sea. But I suppose asylum seekers are good for the hotel trade – or what's left of it,' muttered Boyd.

'I'm sorry you don't admire Seagate. Let's hope Roma Lorta takes a different view when he goes there to speak to his people.'

'As a terrorist from some God-forsaken Balkan state? I don't know why they're letting him into the country,' said Boyd sourly.

'The British government want Lorta to be seen as a freedom fighter.'

'Well, they would, wouldn't they?'

'The British government want to see him in power.'

'Whatever for?'

'He's a pussy cat,' said Creighton. 'Open to UN demands, unlike so many others. But as you know, we've got intelligence that he could be assassinated.'

'Isn't he on a national goodwill tour? Why Seagate? There's no goodwill there.'

'But there's a large number of refugees from Lubic. If Lorta's in power they might feel safe enough to go back there. That's what we want. That's what Lorta says he wants.'

'But others don't?'

'There's an equally high number of refugees who'd just like him dead.'

'So why the robbery?' Boyd spoke in a monotone, merciful numbness spreading. 'What was the fucking point?'

'We've been through all this,' said Creighton patiently. 'The raid was to signal a professional.' He paused. 'There's a shortage of professionals. What did Patterson tell you?'

'That I'm a cheap little bastard from London who's done

time and lost his family. So far accurate enough.' Boyd was bitter.

'Did he tell you that your alias, Rick James, is a born-again Christian?'

'Good grief! Patterson certainly kept that bit to himself. How did Rick get to be one of those?' Boyd looked alarmed.

'Saw the light.'

'I see. And what is Rick going to do with the light?'

'He's going right round to see the Seekers.'

'Who the hell are they?'

'They're a small charity based in Seagate that helps support the asylum seekers. Counselling and legal advice – that kind of thing.'

'So Rick can work for God?'

'Actually you'll be working for a small-time police informer called George Hanley. He manages the charity.'

'What will he know about me?'

'Nothing. But's he's got an eye for talent. He uses his position at Seekers – at least we think he does.'

'How?'

'He could be setting up asylum seekers as criminals. No one's sure.'

'Works on both sides of the fence, does he? Petty crime?'

'So far. But Hanley could well get higher aspirations and have them robbing banks.'

'Am I meant to be his inspiration?'

'You should be. After all, you just made a successful raid.'

'With appalling results.'

'That won't put Hanley off. He taps in everywhere. Gives the local police titbits about the asylum seekers. The stuff he wants to give, of course. Nothing more, nothing less.'

'But you don't know where he's at?'

'DI Faraday, your contact in Seagate CID, has a few ideas. But we need an insider.'

'So Rick doesn't really believe in God.'

'Ostensibly he does.'

'But in reality he's rooting for himself.'

'Yes.'

Boyd paused, trying to assess the information, but his thoughts were still dominated by what he'd done. With considerable effort he returned to the subject in hand. 'What's the set-up at Seekers?'

'It's a registered charity with a board of trustees.'

'Squeaky clean?'

'Nothing known against them,' said Creighton.

'And you reckon Hanley could also be recruiting for an assassination attempt. What would he get out of that?'

'A lot of money.'

'From what source?'

'Interested parties.'

'Or could he be out to stop the assassination?'

'Anything's possible.'

'So you want me to find out. And you reckon the bank raid gave me sufficient credibility.'

There was a fractional pause before Creighton replied.

'Some,' he said at last.

'Where's the proceeds of the robbery?'

'The local police will get a tip-off that the cash is stashed away in a remote farmhouse.'

'Doesn't that rather undermine my credibility?'

'No – you did the job. The mistake would be seen to be made by your employers.'

'And the child?'

'Hanley won't be bothered about that.' Creighton got up and the bedsprings creaked. 'I'm not totally insensitive.'

'You could fool me.'

'I know what you've been through.'

'Don't give me that shit.'

'Ever since, you've buried yourself in your work – in your aliases. You've got to do that again. For your own safety as well as ours.' Creighton was adamant.

'You don't think the boy is a little close to home?'

19

'It was unfortunate.'

'Should I admit what I did to Hanley?'

'Yes – and that will be the end of it.'

'Or just the beginning,' suggested Boyd warily.

Creighton gazed at him steadily and then lowered his eyes. 'Do you want to be taken out?'

For a moment Boyd wanted to say yes, that he did, that to be taken out would be for the best. Then he remembered the empty house where nothing happened but the reliving of his loss. And now he would have a much more recent memory burnt into his mind.

'I'll stay in,' said Boyd. 'You know I can't afford to get out.'

'Try and keep as stable as you can,' said Creighton. 'If you don't, although you may not want out I could be forced to pull you. Meanwhile we'll keep in very close touch. I want you to talk to me regularly. Like every day – on your mobile.'

'That's not usual procedure,' muttered Boyd.

'It is now,' replied Creighton.

Edina Milstein sat in Rila's room, hugging her.

The tiny space seemed packed with photographs of Stefan, smiling down from every surface and wall, and Edina was finding his gaze increasingly oppressive. She wanted to help Rila, but all she could do was hold her. Edina could find no words of comfort.

'He was a bad man, a robber. He ran over my darling – he didn't care.'

Edina held her closer. Tears poured down Rila's stained cheeks.

'I might as well go home. I've got nothing. I'm alone.'

'You'd be alone in Kosovo,' Edina told her. 'Alone – and in danger.'

'I have friends –'

'You have friends here. More friends. Make your life here.'

'I'll stay by his grave.'

'You have to go where they send you.'

Rila pulled away, not able to bear Edina's stark realism, but Edina only pulled her back in a tighter hug than before.

Chapter Three

That night Boyd dreamt he was hurtling down the M25 in a green van. The front seat of the vehicle was spacious enough to take all five of them. His own family, Rick, Mary and Abbie, were sitting, staring ahead, while next to Abbie was the boy with the rucksack. They were travelling at far too great a speed, and the van was rocking violently when Boyd woke to find himself in a sixties high-rise block of flats in Seagate.

He checked his watch, took two Disprin for a stinging headache and turned on the television news. He had to wait some time for the regional items, and even then they put the snowstorms before the news of the boy's death.

'A ten-year-old boy died, run over by the getaway van after two armed men had threatened security guards and stolen over £250,000 outside the HSBC bank in Audley Square, Seagate. The raid happened during a snowstorm, and it is thought that the getaway driver skidded on the slippery road surface. The boy, who has been named as Stefan Kovac, died immediately. He was on his way home from school. His mother, Rila Kovac, was with her son only moments after the accident. The police found the getaway vehicle abandoned in a cliff car park a mile up the coast. They also found the stolen money, after a tip-off, in a derelict farmhouse near Steyning. The driver of the van is being sought, along with another man. The police are asking for any witnesses to come forward, but advise the public not to approach these men as they are both armed and dangerous.'

Boyd flicked off the TV, looked in an empty fridge and then remembered he would have to shop for food. He'd noticed a café down the road and decided to have breakfast. Oddly enough he felt incredibly hungry.

On his way down in the lift he met an elderly woman, heavily made up, with a shopping bag.

'New here, are you?' she asked flatly.

'Just moved in.'

'Thought you were an unfamiliar face.'

Boyd didn't reply, not wanting to take part in what he was sure was going to be an intrusive conversation. But he also knew he had no choice.

'Half the tenants have left,' the woman said in grim delight. 'This place is going to be torn down next year.'

'I only want somewhere to stay for a few weeks.'

The doors of the lift opened and they stepped out into the filthy foyer. An old bike, minus a wheel, and a fridge had been dumped there.

'Here to see friends?'

'I've come to do a job.'

She laughed, standing in front of the doors and trapping him. 'A job? In Seagate? Don't make me laugh.'

'I wasn't trying to.'

'Where are you going to get your job?'

'Actually it's voluntary.'

'*What?*' She sounded as if he'd blasphemed.

'I'm going to work for Seekers.'

'Them!' She spat out the word. 'Do-gooders!'

'I'm down from London.'

'Don't you need to work? I mean, get real work?'

'Not for a while.'

'You got money then?'

'Enough for a few months.'

'What happens then?'

'I'll have to find some paid work.'

'What made you turn up in Seagate – of all places?' She was gazing at Boyd as if he was insane.

'God called me.'

'Who?'

'God.' This was his first try and Boyd wondered if this aspect of his background was going to work or whether he would simply be regarded as ludicrous. Why had Creighton included this burden on his identity? Then he remembered Creighton enlarging on the theme. 'We need you to have a reason for voluntary work,' he had told him. 'And this was the best we could find.'

'You're one of them.'

'How do you mean?'

'Do-gooders.' The woman seemed exasperated. 'Well, I don't want to know. Bloody asylum seekers. I don't know about God. I reckon they worship the devil.'

'Well, I must be getting on.' Boyd tried to dodge round her, but she was still blocking his way.

'So we're neighbours then.'

Boyd resigned himself. He couldn't afford to upset the neighbours. Even if he had killed a child. A voice inside him began to ask which was the worse crime.

'And so are the asylum seekers. That's why the charity I'm going to work for was set up,' he said firmly.

'Bloody charities,' she spat out. 'I reckon charity begins at home. I mean –' She looked witheringly at him. 'Why should I have to live in this dump?'

'Can't you get better accommodation?'

'I've been here thirty years. They'll have to carry me out feet first.'

Boyd tried to redress his tactical error. 'You mean the council should refurbish the place.'

'How can they refurbish it if the flats're going to be demolished?' She looked at him accusingly and Boyd realized he'd made yet another mistake.

What was the matter with him? But of course he knew. It was the boy.

Then his unwanted companion hurried on. 'Of course they *say* they're going to demolish the place. But I reckon they'll put the decision off again.'

'Probably.'

'And there's another thing . . .'

'What's that?'

'You say you're out to help them asylum seekers . . .'

'If I can.'

'Well, one of their kids got killed yesterday. In that bank job,' she added with dramatic glee. Boyd winced and then tried to meet her gimlet eye. 'You going to help his mum, are you?'

'If I can.'

'What will you do? Bring her to God?'

Boyd needed to end the conversation. 'I'm glad we're neighbours,' he said. 'My name's Rick James.' Too late he realized with sudden irony that his alias was the name of his dead son. Could Creighton have done that deliberately?

'I'm Sheila Morton,' she said, and they achieved a cold handshake. 'You must come in and have a drink sometime, or don't you drink – being a Holy Joe?'

'I'm not a priest, Sheila.'

'Just a God bod.' She gave a grating laugh, but still refused to move. 'You're upset about that boy, aren't you?'

'I'm upset about all of them.' How did she know? Had he given himself away?

'But what can you do?'

'Bring comfort.'

'Trying to convert them, are you? They're all heathens.'

'They're largely Muslims. I'm not attempting to convert anyone. I respect their religion. Christ and Mohammed have a lot in common. In fact they spring from the same root.'

With some pleasure Boyd could see that his earnest morality had satisfactorily terminated the conversation, and that she no longer wished to interrogate him. Sheila Morton stood aside and watched him leave, getting stuck in the badly revolving door because he had become so self-conscious.

His flat, in a run-down block, was some streets away from Audley Square. He was glad of that. Nevertheless, the boy was on his mind all the time – whether he was asleep or awake. And as if what had happened wasn't bad enough, surely the crowning irony had to be to make him a born-again Christian. Boyd inwardly cursed Creighton. He had no idea how to handle the role – as he had just proved in his conversation with Sheila Morton.

Mortified, Boyd hurried towards the café. Then he saw him, walking slowly up the road.

'Forty-forty,' said the nutter and doffed a rancid-looking cap.

He's all I need, thought Boyd as he watched the man walk away, clasping his football in his raised right hand.

Somehow the mentally ill seemed symbolic of the very spirit of Seagate. How could such a worn-out, wasted and unsupported place ever offer comfort to asylum seekers? *'Trying to convert them, are you? They're all heathens.'* Sheila Morton's words rang mockingly in his ears.

After breakfast, Boyd arrived on the Seagate promenade. Once, he thought, Seagate must have been not only attractive but actually elegant. At one end was a large, ornate and rusting pier and, at the other, a long jetty that thrust out into the sea. All along the promenade there were gilded lamp posts with empty hanging baskets, and tracks showed that some kind of sightseeing railway line had once existed, although there was no sign of it now.

Set back behind a wide road were a series of turreted buildings, once obviously smart hotels but now darkly rotting. Most of their names had been removed, unlike the Grand Hotel, which still had broken lettering across its canopy and retained a distinct air of faded grandeur.

The guest houses that followed the line of hotels seemed

to be in better condition, newly painted, with names like Mon Repos, Dunroamin and, inevitably, Sea View.

Mounds of grey snow were piled up against the railings of the promenade, and as he made his way along, Boyd had to watch his step. There were a number of concrete shelters looking out to sea, full of men and women, hunched in their coats, apathetically staring out at the grey horizon. They certainly weren't British and most had Slavic features. There was no sign of any children and Boyd wondered if they had been kept indoors, out of the way of skidding vans.

Outside a newsagent's was a placard that read CHILD KILLED IN BANK RAID, and a shaft of ice seemed to find its way into his heart. A wave of self-loathing swept through him, and he stopped and leant on the railings that separated the promenade from the beach and thought about the job he did for Creighton. It was a job that constantly changed his identity and plunged him into one dangerous situation after another, but not caring about his own life, Boyd had been glad to shelter in anonymity. He desperately needed to wipe out the memory of the death of his wife and children, his best loved, his only loved, because he'd been driving too fast and too carelessly all those years ago.

So now he had to make regular contact with Creighton. Boyd knew he was no longer trusted. He also knew that he could be pulled – and then it would be back to Sutton and a long-empty house that still held searingly painful echoes.

He hurried on towards the pier, realizing he would be late for his appointment with Hanley. Not a good start, he thought. But of course a much worse start had already been made. He could see the boy somersaulting, school books bursting out of his rucksack and still falling as he went under the wheels of the green van.

Boyd would always remember the soft bump as he drove over the boy – and then sped on, while Patterson talked him down. Christ knew how he was going to live with this. The dangerous world of the insider had once been his comfort. Now that comfort was over.

The word SEEKERS was crudely written on the window of a shop that was part of the front of the pier and was encrusted with complicated plaster scrolls, most of which had crumbled away, while the few remaining spelt out the legend BEACH TEAS.

Boyd rattled at the front door and then rang the bell.

The door was eventually opened by a tall man with a pale oval face and a beard, carefully dressed in a dark suit, white shirt and highly polished black shoes. He had a slight stoop and the only concession to colour was a large and surprisingly brash tie.

'George Hanley?'

'Yes.'

'I'm Rick James.'

'Do come in.' His voice was deep and brown, with a distinctive middle-class accent that Boyd knew belonged to the southern commuter belt. An unlikely candidate for an informer – or was he just stereotyping informers?

Hanley led Boyd through a small untidy office into a larger room, equally untidy, with a couple of armchairs that were covered in magazines, largely of a political nature. Hanley pushed them to the floor and Boyd did the same, sitting down awkwardly, realizing that he had not been expecting this rather distinguished elderly man.

'I'm sorry for the mess,' said Hanley. 'Regrettably, I've never had a sense of order and I'm too old to acquire one now.'

This distinctive figure would stand out anywhere, thought Boyd. How could a criminal confide in him?

'Tell me about yourself,' invited Hanley.

'It's not a pretty tale.'

'I'm sure I've heard worse.'

'I've been inside. Before that I had a job as a car salesman. I also had a family.'

'Why were you serving time?'

'Fraud. But, before that –'

'Any sex offences?' asked Hanley. He wasn't in the least embarrassed. It was almost as if he was asking Boyd whether he drank tea with or without sugar and milk.

'No.'

'I've already had you checked on the register.'

Then why ask? thought Boyd with a spurt of anger.

'And what about your family?'

'My marriage broke up. I don't see my wife – or my children. She's done everything she can to keep me away from them.' Boyd paused. 'When I was in the Scrubs I had a series of dreams, revelations even.' Here came the test, but Boyd had already devoted much thought to it while he ate breakfast.

Hanley nodded gravely.

'I saw myself walking hand-in-hand with a stranger. We climbed a mountain and looked down into the next valley. There was a lake – and in its glittering surface I saw glimpses of my life so far. I was disgusted. I looked again at my guide. I was still holding his hand. Then I realized he was Jesus Christ, the Son of God.' Boyd paused. So far he had avoided eye contact with Hanley. Surely that was a mistake? He looked up at him, but Hanley's face held no expression although he seemed to be taking him seriously. 'I'm sure all this sounds crazy.' Despite the cold Boyd was sweating, wondering if his badly concocted and facile-sounding story was just about passing muster.

'Not at all,' said Hanley politely.

'Anyway, I decided to change my life. To give back.'

'To make a difference?' asked Hanley gently.

Boyd winced and continued his tale. 'I've got some savings and I decided to get out of London, to come here. I'd heard about the charity.'

'Where?' demanded Hanley, his voice suddenly crisp.

'I can't remember. In a newspaper. Maybe on TV,' Boyd improvised.

Hanley nodded. 'We've had more than our share of publicity. But usually of the wrong kind.'

'No doubt. But this wasn't hostile – on the contrary. So I decided to offer my services – for as long as I can last on my savings.'

'It's difficult work.'

'I'm sure.'

'But there could be a chance of a job with a reasonable salary here. We may be going to receive additional funding.'

'Surely you'd need a qualified social worker at that stage –'

'I'm not sure I'd want a qualified social worker. I need someone to effectively interact with our client group.' He sounded pompous, the jargon stiff and self-conscious.

'Do you have someone like that in mind?'

'Not at the moment. Several people have tried, but they've all left – largely because the work is difficult and demoralizing. Also the money we're able to offer at present is minimal.' He paused. 'I took a cut in salary to provide money for an additional paid worker.' He sounded mildly heroic.

'Do you have other volunteers?'

'Not now. They've all fallen away. I've been trying to handle some of our cases myself, but I have to spread myself far too thin.'

'I'd have expected Seekers to attract a lot of volunteers,' said Boyd tentatively.

'Asylum seekers aren't popular. This isn't a cause célèbre.'

'So you'll take me on?'

'If you want to give it a try.'

'Thank you.' Boyd was interested. He seemed to have been brought on board too easily. Was this unlikely police informer aiming to manipulate him? And what were the chances of Hanley coming clean? Would he play his cards close to his chest, or would he attempt to draw Rick James in? And did Hanley know all about the raid with its disastrous outcome?

'One thing,' said Hanley.

'What's that?' Boyd was tense.

'I can't allow you to preach to our clients.'

'I never had any intention of doing so.' Boyd made himself sound slightly offended. 'I believe God called me to do this work. But I'm not going to evangelize.'

'I thought that was the duty of a born-again Christian?'

'That's not my own belief. If someone is ready to come to God then I'll show them the way as best I can. But that's the limit.'

'Very well,' said Hanley. 'I'll accept your word on this. And I have to tell you that I'm an atheist – and always have been.'

Boyd wondered if Creighton had more inside information than he had given him. Did Hanley have some kind of Achilles heel as far as religion went?

Boyd nodded. 'I respect your position.'

'Really?' Hanley sounded surprised. 'You're a bit of an oddball for a born-again Christian, aren't you? I would have thought you'd have risen to the challenge.'

'I'm my own man.' Vaguely Boyd wondered if he'd made a mistake and been caught out. He couldn't seem to make up his mind. 'Tell me more about the asylum seekers,' he said quickly.

'They're angry and humiliated. Some have been here for a couple of years, waiting to see if they can receive British nationality. Others arrived more recently. They're given little or no information about the progress of their applications and live in depressing conditions in a bleak town that doesn't want them. Seagate is one of many of course, but arguably more run-down than some.'

'And their countries of origin?'

'The former Yugoslavia, Iraq, Iran, and now Afghanistan.'

31

'Have they lost touch with their families?'

'In some cases their families have been wiped out. In others, it's all a question of buying telephone cards and using whatever public telephones are available to call home.'

'And they're on benefit?'

'Of course. And this is deeply resented by the locals. But these asylum seekers have come from hell at home – and they expected to be treated at least with dignity. In fact they're treated like fifth-class citizens at best – or, at worst, criminals.'

'Have they committed crimes?'

'Some – out of desperation.'

And will you be helping them to commit more crime and on a much larger scale, wondered Boyd, or was Hanley genuine? But that still left his role as police informer a mystery.

Boyd decided to go more gently. 'Do you have a board of trustees?'

'Local worthies.'

'Who are sympathetic –'

'They don't have to get their hands dirty. Our president is Harry Day, who was a Labour councillor here, and our chairperson is Hilary Browning, the former Conservative MP who lost her seat at the last election.'

'So they're both from the front line.'

'Very much so, but they're hard-working.'

'What would I be expected to do?' asked Boyd, still treading carefully.

'Explain their rights to the asylum seekers. Support families. Help out with disputes –'

'I've no training for that.'

'I have. And I can advise you. In the meantime I suggest you do some reading.' He got up and pulled down a tatty-looking manual entitled *Asylum Seekers: Their Rights*.

'Thank you,' said Boyd. 'This will be interesting.' He paused. 'When do I start?'

'Spend the rest of the day taking a look round the town. Then come and see me the same time tomorrow. Harry Day and Hilary Browning will be here.'

'So you are taking me on?'

'But not God as well,' Hanley reminded him.

Chapter Four

Boyd spent the rest of the day walking the streets of Seagate, eventually forcing himself to return to Audley Square.

A bitter salt wind blew off the English Channel, but the snow was so hard the frozen mounds barely stirred. Boyd trudged towards the square apprehensively, looking neither to left nor right, walking towards the Grand Hotel and pausing. He gazed up at the once noble exterior with its snow-laden canopy above the dirty marble steps, floor after floor of windows, most of them broken and covered with cardboard, newspaper and even towels to keep out the cold. The vast hulk seemed like a stranded liner, about to sink.

Could people really live in that rat-hole? Risking challenge, Boyd walked into the foyer to marvel at the great sweep of the central staircase, now covered in litter, a supermarket trolley hanging at a crazy angle from the topmost stair. The effect was surreal. In the foyer, the reception counter still curved round the right-hand side of the staircase, but was now covered with broken boxes and old newspapers. To the left of the staircase was what had once been the hall porter's desk where theatre tickets might have been bought. There was even part of a damp-stained poster advertising an ice show at the local rink. Two lifts were marked DO NOT ATTEMPT TO USE and above a gaping hole in the floorboards was a sign DANGER – UNSAFE FLOOR. The sign seemed to be stating the obvious.

Boyd was just about to turn away and go outside again when someone hailed him from the stairs.

'Excuse me. Can I help you?' The young man was short, with Slavic features, wearing a cap and an overcoat that was huge and thick and completely swamped him. Boyd guessed it was some kind of hand-out from a charity shop.

'I'm sorry,' said Boyd. 'I was just being nosy about the building. I love its state of magnificent decay.'

'It's getting worse than that,' he replied in heavily accented English. 'The place is falling apart.'

Boyd backed away. 'Sorry for trespassing.'

'You don't have to apologize.'

'I'm going to work for Seekers – the charity.' Boyd felt he was blurting out the words clumsily.

'They're good,' said the man with a rather false enthusiasm, obviously being careful not to offend a possible source of help. 'Or at least – they try,' he added more honestly.

'Do you live here?'

'Yes. I have done for some months. My name is Djuro Nemenescu. My middle name is Stefan,' he added and paused, as if for effect. 'I have the same name as the little boy who was killed coming home from school. Killed by the bank robbers.'

'Yes. I heard about the tragedy on the news.' Boyd realized he was trembling and fought for self-control.

'His mother is distraught.'

Boyd cursed himself for ever setting foot inside the Grand. 'Of course.'

'It is particularly unfortunate that she is alone now. All she had was Stefan. The rest of her family are dead. She worshipped him.'

'Maybe I can help her.' Boyd heard himself say the words that he had been fighting back.

'Would you like to meet her?'

Boyd hesitated.

'She's in her room now. Other women are with her.'

'Maybe I should wait until tomorrow – when I'm actually starting my job at Seekers.'

'What makes you want to do this work?' The young man was closer now and suddenly sounded aggressive.

'I'd heard of the plight the asylum seekers were in, and I wanted to be useful.'

The answer seemed to mollify Nemenescu. 'That's good of you,' he said, and then added, 'But why?'

Boyd's mind raced. Anything he revealed now would be remembered and could go against him, particularly born-again Christianity.

'I've been so bored by the work I did in London.'

'What was that?'

More mind racing. 'I was a delivery driver. I had this van. I grew to hate that van.'

Nemenescu laughed and Boyd felt a rush of confidence.

'I had my own farm. Well – it was small, but, yes – a farm.'

'Where was this?'

'Bosnia. I think you would call it a market garden. But when the war came we had to go – or we'd have been killed. By the neighbours.'

'Did your family survive?'

'Fortunately, yes. My wife and two sons and my father. We all came here. Now we are living in what you might call a rabbit hutch, and we wait – for citizenship. Maybe we wait for ever.'

'It must be very hard to occupy your time.'

'We have a set routine. My wife and I walk the streets in the morning. Then we come back and make lunch. In the afternoon we walk the streets again. After that we make supper. We all eat in front of a small TV screen and we're lucky to have that. Each day we have the same routine. We look forward to going to bed, to dream about home.'

'Do you want to go back there?'

'We can't.'

The reply didn't invite further questions, but Boyd found himself floundering on.

'And your father?'

'He is not well. So he stays in – and watches the TV screen all day. He tells me he is absorbing the British language. He speaks fluent French and Spanish.'

'Your English is good.'

'That is because my mother was a linguist too. She and my father were translators.'

'Have you been to England before?'

'Never.'

'What do you think of it?'

'I've seen a little bit of London, and a great deal of Seagate. But Seagate is not a great deal, is it?'

They both laughed and the atmosphere on the staircase grew less tense. Boyd asked him, 'Your mother is still in Bosnia?'

'No. She died many years ago.'

'I'm very sorry.'

'Don't let me keep you.' Nemenescu sounded dismissive now.

'I've enjoyed talking to you,' Boyd persisted. 'I hope to see you again.' He paused. 'Your English is so good I'm wondering if you're up to a colloquialism.'

'Try me.'

'As far as I can see, everyone in Seagate who is an asylum seeker is up shit creek.'

Nemenescu smiled. 'I understand your colloquialism. Maybe we could have a drink together sometime.'

'That would be a pleasure.'

As Nemenescu went back upstairs, Boyd realized rather too late that 'up shit creek' was hardly the sort of colloquialism a born-again Christian would use.

As Boyd came out of the Grand he saw the piles of flowers in the snow. Several passers-by had paused to gaze at them, and as he came up an elderly man was talking to an elderly woman. They were both shabbily dressed.

As Boyd paused with considerable pain to look at

the flowers, he couldn't avoid overhearing their conversation.

'He was only ten,' she was saying.

'Seagate's seen better days,' the elderly man replied rather enigmatically.

But Boyd found a personal meaning in his tired phrase. You can say that again, he thought. The irony of his presence there was intensely painful. What the hell would the old couple say if they knew the boy's killer was standing beside them?

'That's an understatement,' she snapped. 'First the unemployment, second the asylum seekers, then the crime wave, and now the terrible bank raid and the murder of that child.'

'The child of an asylum seeker.'

'A child nevertheless,' she snapped again. 'An innocent child. This town is worse than London.'

'Or New York,' her companion added with enthusiasm.

'It's terrible, isn't it?' she said to Boyd.

He nodded, still gazing down at the flowers, feeling unutterably trapped.

'Are you local?' she demanded.

'Just for a while.'

'But you didn't know Seagate in its heyday.'

'I'm afraid not.'

'I was born here,' she continued, and Boyd felt her dignity. 'My father was the local doctor. Seagate was a lovely place before the war, elegant and charming. Now it's dying – like I am.'

The elderly man tried to be gallant. 'I'm sure you've got many more years in you yet, Edith.'

'But I'm not sure I want to live them out. Not here, anyway.' She paused. 'But where else could I go? My parents left me the house, but I've got no money. I can't just up-sticks.'

'You could sell the house.'

'Henry – you know I'd never do a thing like that. They left it to me. Mummy and Daddy.'

Boyd saw that she was close to tears and tried to change the subject. 'Were you born here too?' he asked.

Henry shook his head. 'I've been here since the fifties. My parents bought a linen shop – haberdashery. Drake & Co. A lovely shop and I took it on for a while after Dad died. But the place was too old-fashioned and like Edith I had no money to make changes. Drake & Co closed ten years ago. Now the building's an amusement arcade where the asylum seekers hang around all day. Edith's right. Seagate died a long time ago. There's no life here.'

'But it still has a large population,' volunteered Boyd and there was an awkward silence.

'I'm not a racist,' said Edith.

'And neither am I,' added Henry. 'But why did they have to come here?'

Boyd wandered the streets for the next hour, taking in Seagate. In some ways there was a chill charm to the Edwardian promenade, the weathered pier with its rusty iron girders, the crumbling jetty, the rows of beach huts with their peeling paint, the faded amusement park, the boarded-up ice-cream kiosks and a milk bar that hadn't changed since the fifties, the near derelict hotels and the battered sign near the jetty which read SEAGATE – YOUR BRIGHT AND BREEZY RESORT.

In a sense Boyd knew the legend was still true. A tepid sun had come out, brilliantly lighting the town's mantle of snow, and a freezing cold wind was coming off the sea, waves pounding the pebble beach, sending spray up on to the promenade.

'Who's a cheeky boy?' asked a mechanical parrot with mind-blowing repetition from its perch above the amusement arcade, and Boyd was forcibly reminded of Hamlet, the parrot which he had taken home from one of his cases and then passed on to a neighbour. The arcade was packed with men, many of whom looked Slavic. None of them were playing the machines, but they were all intently gazing at them as if their gaudy lights and rattling sounds were an escape from the wasteland around them.

Then in another arcade a little further down the promenade an argument broke out as a slight young man was physically ejected.

'If you're not going to spend money,' the burly bouncer yelled, 'get out and stay out!'

'This cold,' shouted the young man in uncertain English. 'Too cold to be on the street.' He was certainly inadequately dressed, with a dirty T-shirt and jeans, a scarf wound round his neck.

Boyd felt a rush of anger. For God's sake, surely the asylum seekers had suffered enough in their own country not to be rejected yet again.

'Hang on,' Boyd said, knowing that it was a mistake to intercede, but not able to stop himself. He dug a fiver out of his pocket and gave it to the young man who looked surprised – as if he didn't know what to do with the money.

But before he could react, the bouncer turned on Boyd. 'Don't give them any fucking money.'

'Now he can play your machines and stay warm.'

'I don't want him in here.'

'What's he done wrong?'

'He hangs around.'

'And what's wrong with that?'

'They don't spend money. None of them do.'

Drained and exhausted, Boyd lost his temper. 'Well, now he's *got* some fucking money.'

'I don't want them here,' said the bouncer truculently, 'and neither does my boss.'

'What's your name?'

'I'm not giving you any name. Who the hell do you think you are? Now fuck off out of it – both of you.'

'I insist that you allow him back in.' Boyd knew he was becoming pompous.

'You fucking well –'

'No,' said the young man. 'I don't want to go back in. And I don't want your money.' He threw Boyd's fiver on the ground and spat on it.

The bouncer and Boyd stared at the money in some confusion as the young man walked away.

When he was out of sight down a side street, Boyd said, 'Don't you have any sensitivity?'

'What about?'

'These people.'

'I'm up to here with them. They rob and cheat and take over. The place is packed with them.'

Boyd saw that the men in the arcade were beginning to move out to stand on the pavement around them, curious at the outcome of the conflict. Realizing he had made a fool of himself, Boyd began to back off. 'I haven't got time for this.'

Then Boyd heard an all too familiar voice. 'Forty-forty,' said the nutter. 'Forty-forty.' Slipping his football under his arm he bent down and picked up the fiver.

Boyd and the bouncer gazed at each other as if the sudden intervention had thrown them both and turned their mutual hostility upside down.

'So you give away money, do you?' sneered the bouncer.

'Occasionally,' replied Boyd.

The gathering crowd began to retreat back into the amusement arcade, realizing the main action was over.

'Forty-forty,' said the nutter. 'Forty-forty.'

'Shut the fuck up,' snarled the bouncer.

The spire of the church dominated downtown Seagate which, beyond the promenade, petered out into boarded-up shops, a pub and a tatty-looking betting shop. But when Boyd came upon the church in a quiet square there was no sense of tawdriness at all. It was almost as if he had arrived in another town that was prosperous and well maintained.

The church was Gothic and in some indefinable way exuded a brooding authority, as if the building was a bastion of strength that only the pure of heart could enter. Boyd had the curious thought that he had been brought to the church for a reason, and tried to work out why such a thought had entered his mind unbidden.

The square was cobbled, with a warehouse on one side and a block of flats on the other. Around the church was a carefully maintained graveyard.

Boyd walked towards the porch, expecting the door to be locked. Instead it opened and he walked inside. The interior was dark and smelt of incense, candle grease and furniture polish, and he walked slowly across the tiled floor and sat in a pew at the back, looking at the twelve Stations of the Cross, the plaster saints, the banks of candles and the much larger statue of the Virgin Mary with the child Jesus in her arms. She was gazing ahead at a pallid sunbeam shining through the coloured glass, focusing on the worn stone floor.

Rick, he thought. Rick James. Creighton wouldn't have done that deliberately. He had his own integrity. Suddenly tears came into Boyd's eyes as he remembered his dead son and the boy he had killed – the two boys he had killed – as well as the rest of his family. Try as he might to force the memories away they came back relentlessly, while the tears flooded down his cheeks.

He knew the church was Catholic, but what did that matter? He'd never had a religion, but now in this bleak place he suddenly wished he had. Five years ago now, yet their deaths were as painful as if they had happened yesterday. Like the boy.

Boyd saw a priest behind the altar and decided to kneel down, to put his head in his hands, to avoid letting his grief be observed.

As he knelt, the unfamiliar tears continued to pour down his cheeks, and Boyd realized with a shock that he had rarely cried for any of them. He had simply slipped from identity to identity at Creighton's behest, and had brought each investigation to a conclusion. When he wasn't working, when he wasn't safely hidden in an alias, Danny Boyd had returned to the family house in Sutton, as if in a time warp, drinking himself regularly into oblivion and longing for Creighton to find him another case, another persona. His grief had been on hold for too long, but for some strange reason the Church of St Augustine had given him the opportunity to face the pain, to really let it bite.

Then he heard a familiar voice. 'Forty-forty,' declared the nutter as he got to his feet a few pews away, the football balanced in his raised right hand. 'Forty-forty.'

The nutter began to move away from the pew, heading towards the door of the church, eyes glazed.

The priest hurried down the nave to try and catch up with him.

'Hello, Arthur,' he said. 'How are you?'

'Forty-forty,' the madman intoned.

'Do you have accommodation?'

'Forty-forty. No one cares.' Arthur raised two fingers of one hand and the football in the other.

Chapter Five

Boyd got up from his knees and sat in the pew. He felt dazed but no longer drained. He looked at his watch and saw that he had been kneeling for half an hour, yet he hadn't noticed the time passing.

He could no longer see the priest.

Boyd put his head in his hands, wiping away the tears.

Then he sensed someone by his side and jumped.

'I didn't mean to startle you.'

Boyd said nothing. He felt as if the priest had somehow worked a flanker on him. Immediately he was on the defensive. The feeling was familiar.

'If you'd rather I went away that's fine.'

Another ruse, thought Boyd. 'I can't talk.' All his senses told him that he could be trapped into exposing Danny Boyd rather than keeping up the pretence of Rick James.

'You don't have to.' The priest smiled. 'I'm just establishing contact.'

'Like you did with that nutter?'

'Arthur? He's a schizophrenic and an alcoholic. He finds safety here.'

'But he doesn't want to talk to you?'

'He has his own way.'

'This is a terrible town,' said Boyd spontaneously, dropping his guard and then panicking because he had inexplicably done so. 'This church is the only haven I've found. Like Arthur. I gave him a fiver a bit earlier tonight. I suppose I shouldn't have if he's an alcoholic.'

'You weren't to know,' said the priest. 'Of course Seagate's become a dumping ground. You can't make a community out of a dumping ground.'

'You mean the asylum seekers –'

'No. Not just those poor devils. Seagate is the end of the road for a lot of people. Literally at the end of the line.'

'You mean Arthur and –'

'He's not the only one who's come to the end. The town was already going downhill ten years ago when I first took over here; it's just getting worse.' The priest's voice wasn't hushed in the echoing space. 'Now it's like a spluttering fuse.'

'About to blow?'

'I'm worried about this Lorta visit.'

'In what way?'

'He has some followers. He also has enemies.'

'I thought he was a puppet of the British government.'

'Quite so.'

'I heard one of the asylum seekers' children was killed yesterday,' Boyd blurted out and immediately could have kicked himself. Was he seeking some kind of hysterical absolution?

'It was a tragedy. I shall be conducting the funeral, of course.'

'Aren't they Muslim?'

'A lot of the asylum seekers are. But some are Catholic. Some of them even come to church.' The priest paused. 'It's catching, isn't it? Now even I'm referring to them as "them", keeping them depersonalized as if they're the enemy.'

'Some people do see them as the enemy.'

'They use them as scapegoats. They're at the bottom of the pile. All we need is a sex offenders' hostel and *they'll* be at the bottom of the pile. The asylum seekers will move up a bit while everyone unites against another perceived enemy.'

'It was terrible about that boy.' Boyd felt forced to bring up the subject again.

'He was an innocent.'

'Do they know who did it?'

'Seems to have been some kind of bank raid.' The priest sounded uninterested. 'Are you sure I can't help you?'

Boyd shook his head.

'Are you new to the town?'

'Yes.'

'May I know your name?'

'Rick James. I've come to work at Seekers.'

'Why did you decide to do that?' said the priest, the sudden probe taking Boyd by surprise.

'I lost my wife and children.'

'So you're making a fresh start.'

Boyd looked at him sharply, detecting irony in the priest's voice. 'I start tomorrow.'

'Then I expect I'll be seeing something of you.'

'Do you liaise with them?'

'Our paths naturally cross.'

Boyd rose to his feet and the priest moved back as he edged his way stiffly out of the pew.

'I'm Father Tristan.'

They shook hands and Boyd muttered something about seeing him again soon.

'I hope so.'

Boyd was conscious of Father Tristan's eyes on him as he hurried out of St Augustine's.

'I'll kill him,' said Rila.

Edina Milstein and the bereaved mother were standing in Jordan's Funeral Parlour looking down at Stefan. They were both Catholic and it had been tacitly agreed that Edina would help with the arrangements.

Stefan had been cleaned up and there was a serene expression on his face. He lay in the coffin, now dressed in his blue sweater, hands crossed over his chest, eyes delicately closed as if in a light sleep.

By a miracle his face was unmarked, his snub nose and

full lips looking rather like the kitsch watercolours of children at play that hung around the funeral parlour. His lustrous black hair flowed on to his shoulders.

Edina knelt on one side of the coffin and Rila on the other. Holy musak was in the background, distorted by a warped tape.

'Don't torture yourself.'

'I need to.'

'Try to be at peace.'

'How can I?'

'For Stefan's sake.'

'This damned country. It's like being suspended in time. And everywhere is so ugly.'

'Maybe it's only Seagate. Other places might be better.'

'They think this is where we belong.'

'It's only a transit camp.'

Rila got up and kissed Stefan's cold cheek. Edina also rose to her feet and did the same.

'Shall I sit with you?'

'Here?'

'I'd like to be with you.'

'Let's go to a bar. Let's get drunk.'

Edina thought that was a good idea.

The following day Boyd arrived at the pier head office of Seekers having had a very bad night's sleep. His conversation with the priest and the death of Stefan had replayed in his mind, over and over again, until they each had their own terrible rhythm.

Hanley opened the door, dressed as formally as the day before. He took Boyd's hand in a hot, dry grasp, his skin so dry it was almost as if he had a fever.

'They're both here,' he said, leading him into the inner office where a slim, fit-looking, clean-shaven middle-aged man sat in a sports jacket, fawn trousers and a plaid tie. Beside him, in almost comic contrast, was a vast woman with a tent-like dress worn under an old jerkin.

'Harry Day,' said Hanley, 'president of our charity, and our chairperson, Hilary Browning, former MP for Seagate.'

They shook hands.

Hanley gestured to a high-backed chair and Boyd sat down, while Hanley perched himself over-casually on the edge of the desk.

'This is Rick, who is prepared to be a badly paid worker for a period.' As if conscious that perching was unseemly, Hanley went and sat down behind his desk. 'I've briefed them on your background.'

Boyd nodded, grateful he didn't have to start all over again.

Day's and Browning's expressions remained neutral.

'We have a staff crisis.' Harry Day spoke almost brusquely. 'We're not a very popular charity. In fact, at the moment George is the only person on our minuscule payroll.'

'We've *had* more staff, of course.' Hanley seemed anxious to defend the situation. 'Even some volunteers.'

'What happened to them?' asked Boyd, knowing they were covering the same ground as they had in his first interview.

'They dropped out. There's so much public concern – or disquiet – over the ever-growing numbers of asylum seekers that to work with them is to become highly unpopular with the indigenous population.'

Boyd nodded and decided to push the vapid conversation on. 'You do know everything about my background, don't you?'

They all nodded, but with a considerable difference of emphasis. Hanley was anxious, Day impatient and Browning trying to show understanding.

Day was first to speak. 'I'm not concerned about your criminal record, Mr James. I'm just worried about your religious belief.'

'In other words, you think I'm going to ram God down everyone's throats.'

'It wouldn't be appropriate,' said Day firmly.

'You're right.' Boyd was irritated by his supercilious manner. 'And I don't intend to discuss God with anyone. I have a right to my own personal belief of course.'

'Naturally,' said Hilary Browning. 'But there's something else. You have no experience of asylum seekers.'

'So we do need to talk about motivation,' said Day.

Boyd realized with depressing certainty that penetrating Seekers would be harder than he'd thought. There now seemed to be every possibility of him failing the interview. Suppose that actually happened? What could he do? What could Creighton do? Why hadn't Hanley told him there could be difficulties?

'How are you operating now?' Boyd asked crisply, needing to take the lead, determined to impress Day at least.

'As a one-man band.' Hanley was cynical. 'I'm overworked, and it's just not possible to cover the ground. A few months ago we at least had four volunteers.'

'What kind of people were they?' asked Boyd.

'They ranged from elderly do-gooders to a man who was only interested in little boys,' said Day. 'You see why we have to be careful.'

'I can see you don't think I'm the kind of person you want working here.' Boyd got to his feet, testing them out and feeling a sense of impending failure.

'Please, sit down, Mr James.' Hilary Browning sounded both motherly and magisterial. It was a compelling combination. 'We are only being realistic.'

'Of course. And surely with my background –' Boyd still needed to keep a grip on the initiative.

'We've had staff from many backgrounds.' Day sounded impatient.

'But we don't have any at all right now.' Hanley looked up at Boyd in some distress. 'I liked your honesty when you came to see me yesterday.'

'It would have been easy to check on my criminal record –'

'Nevertheless, you still told us yourself. Not only about

that, but your beliefs as well. So please bear with us. I think we should take you on as a paid member of staff.'

Boyd gazed at him in surprise. 'Why me?'

There was a short silence.

'I like you,' said Hilary Browning, and Boyd was fleetingly moved by her directness.

'How can you trust me?'

'We can't,' said Day. 'But as Mr Hanley told you when he interviewed you yesterday, we're being given some extra funding and I agree with Mrs Browning that we should give you a chance. You'll be serving a probationary period of course. We can get rid of you immediately if we're not satisfied.'

'Thank you very much. I just want to do something with my life that's useful.' Boyd felt a surge of triumph: he had succeeded in convincing them, at least for the moment.

'There *is* something else.' Day hesitated and glanced at Browning and Hanley who stared back at him blankly. 'We need to put Rick in the picture,' Day insisted. 'If we are going to employ him, we should be absolutely frank.'

Hanley tried to interrupt.

'Let me explain,' Day smoothly continued. 'I'm concerned that some of the asylum seekers are being recruited by criminals, but I only have hunches to go on, nothing specific.'

Hilary Browning looked uneasy. Surely she can't be hearing all this for the first time, Boyd thought. 'I had no idea this was happening,' she said.

'I'm sorry.' Day was smooth and decisive. 'I've been monitoring the situation for some time. Please hear me out, Hilary,' he added hurriedly as Hilary Browning frowned.

'I would have expected to have been told directly you suspected anything like that,' she snapped.

'I'm sorry. Various contacts of mine, and by that I mean in the police and social services, have warned me that groups of asylum seekers appear to be meeting clandestinely. There's a lot of activity. And then there was that raid.'

Boyd waited, glancing at Hilary, hoping he wasn't showing any sign of anxiety or alarm.

'What are the police saying?' she asked.

'Not a lot,' replied Day. 'But Inspector Faraday did tell me he's beginning to wonder if the bank raid was a form of fund-raising.'

'To what end?' asked Boyd, pleased to be getting a crash course on the situation without having to fish for it.

'There's this Lorta visit. Has Mr Hanley explained to you the –'

'Yes,' said Boyd.

'I'm worried something's brewing,' said Day.

'Like what?' asked Hilary Browning.

He shrugged and suddenly got up, offering his hand to Boyd. 'Welcome to Seekers, Mr James,' he said.

Chapter Six

When Day and Browning had gone, Hanley went over to a battered filing cabinet and pulled out a sheaf of papers that had been stapled together.

'Here's some more material about Seekers, its foundation, status as a charity and the more recent case histories of asylum seekers we've assisted in one way or another. Now this sheet lays out the various problems they have had as a group – and still face today.'

'Is there any structure to the asylum seekers?' asked Boyd.

'There hasn't been until recently, but a central council has been formed and the leading members are Mile Kropitz from Albania, Edina Milstein from Lubic, Fitim Kadric from Bosnia and Josif Genzo from Kosovo. You'll hear from them – I'm sure they'll want to meet you.'

'What are they like?'

'They've all been in Seagate for some time. They live at the Grand,' said Hanley shortly.

'What are their backgrounds?'

'They're a cross section. Kropitz was a farmer, I'm not sure about Milstein, but Kadric is an Orthodox priest, and Genzo an ex-army officer. So at least there's a member from the God-squad available to you.'

Boyd decided to be tough. 'I'd prefer you not to knock my religious beliefs.'

Hanley backed off immediately. 'I'm sorry. I didn't mean to be disrespectful.' He paused and then added, 'As you know, I'm an atheist.'

Boyd nodded, not wishing to pursue the discussion further. 'When can I meet these people?'

'I'll organize something,' said Hanley vaguely. There was an awkward silence and then Hanley rushed into speech. 'Look – I've got an idea about a possible first case for you – someone who will need a good deal of support. It was such a terrible –' He stopped abruptly and looked away.

'What is the case?' asked Boyd.

'A woman who has recently lost her son.'

Boyd felt a sense of shock. 'What's her name?' he asked, deliberately casual.

'Rila Kovac.'

'But isn't she –'

'Stefan's mother.'

'So you *are* throwing me in at the deep end.'

'She needs help,' said Hanley. 'But don't give her any Christian charity.'

'Of course I won't.' Inwardly, Boyd was furious. Why couldn't he let it rest?

'Thank you.'

'Or on any other case so you needn't push it.'

'I won't mention the matter again,' said Hanley stiffly.

'So you want me to go and see Mrs Kovac?'

'Yes.'

'Is there a father?'

'Her family are all dead. Only she and Stefan survived. Now Rila has no one.'

'What can I offer her?'

'Some financial support. A small grant. Food and clothing and a listening ear. Tell her we'll try and find out what stage her application's at with the Home Office.'

'Do you know her?'

'I'm afraid not.'

'So I'm cold calling.'

'Very much so.'

'OK,' said Boyd. Again he wondered whether Hanley was going to show his hand. Was the promised agony of the call on Stefan's mother all part of a test, or was Hanley a red herring? Creighton's information had been unusually sketchy, thought Boyd. If the bank raid *had* given him some kind of criminal credibility, then surely someone would come forward and then he'd be in the thick of it.

Suddenly Boyd saw his life as just an unending series of aliases. And now, even one of his aliases was subdividing. From thief to amateur social worker, this time taking in the irony of dealing out death for a second time. I am the hollow man. The words danced to a banal melody in his head. I am the hollow man.

'Have the central council been able to help Rila Kovac?' Hanley looked at him thoughtfully, and Boyd wondered about the length of his silence. 'I'm sure they've been supportive,' he babbled.

'Of course,' said Hanley. 'But like all the other asylum seekers they have nothing material to offer her.'

'When should I go?'

'How about now?'

Boyd paused. 'That's fine by me. But surely my lack of experience isn't going to help. Should I really use a tragedy like this as a learning curve?'

'Why not?' said Hanley. 'We all have to start somewhere.'

Boyd was apprehensive as he approached Audley Square, noting that there were even more flowers heaped on the spot where he had crushed Stefan. Hurrying past them he went quickly into the Grand.

'Do you know where Mrs Kovac lives?' he asked a teenager who was lounging in the foyer, rolling up a cigarette. He shrugged and walked away. Boyd assumed that he either didn't speak English or wasn't prepared to co-operate, or both.

Then he saw an old man coming slowly down the central flight of stairs.

'Excuse me. Do you speak English?'

'Yes, sir.' He was too respectful.

'I'm looking for Mrs Kovac. Rila Kovac.'

'Are you the police?'

'No. I'm here from Seekers.'

'The charity. Have you something to offer her?'

'A small grant.'

He nodded. 'She could use that. You heard about the tragedy?'

'The child.'

'Some bastard robber just mowed her son down. Stefan was all she had.'

Boyd felt as if he was gazing into an open pit. 'Can you tell me where to find her?'

'Up the staircase, on the fifth floor. Number five. And the lifts don't work.'

'Thank you.' He didn't want to prolong the conversation. His inner pain was too great. Boyd hurried up the filthy stairs, shoes clattering on marble.

'Number five, fifth floor. Number five,' the old man called after him, as if Boyd had to be carefully instructed. 'Knock,' he added.

'Of course.'

The staircase curved and the old man was lost to sight. Not that Boyd had looked back. He felt too engrossed in trying to block out Boyd and get into the skin of Rick James. He *had* to be James. The meeting with Rila Kovac would be impossible if Boyd was involved.

Eventually, with a pounding heart that had not been caused by the climb, Boyd came to the fifth floor and stood before number five. The wallpaper along the corridor was hanging off in strips and the dank smell was almost overpowering.

He knocked and waited, knowing that he was barely coping. This had to be the worst case he had ever taken on. Worse still, Boyd was clinging to him. He couldn't reach Rick James, couldn't assume the mantle of the false identity. So what the hell was he going to do?

Eventually the door slowly opened and he saw a woman

with unfashionably plaited brown hair, wearing a cardigan over a blouse and skirt. She looked curiously dated, as if she was in a commercial with a nostalgic fifties background.

'Yes?'

'Mrs Kovac?'

'Yes.' Her monosyllables were uncompromising.

'I'm from Seekers.'

'Your identity . . .?'

Boyd gave her a card and she passed it back, hardly bothering to look at it.

'What do you want?'

'You are entitled to a small grant.'

'From Seekers?'

'Yes.' He was sure he sounded both pompous and patronizing, but inwardly Boyd felt incredibly exposed.

'That is kind.'

Her sudden gratitude made Boyd feel even worse.

'Will you come in?' It was more like a statement than a question.

'Thank you. I shan't keep you long.' Where is James, Boyd screamed inside. Where was the comfort of disguise?

Rila Kovac led Boyd into the rear section of a big room that must once have overlooked the sea but was now divided into two. The space was dingy and box-like, holding two beds and an electric stove, a TV set on a crate and a couple of chairs with springs that seemed to be in the final stages of collapse. The mantelpiece was crowded with pictures, all of a good-looking young boy with a wide Slavic face and long dark hair and a snub nose. There were more pictures of him on the wall. He was half-smiling but his eyes were expressionless. You don't always smile with the eyes, Boyd told himself. But he knew this particular boy would never smile at anyone again.

'Would you like tea?'

'No, thanks.'

'You think I can't make it? We live on the stuff.' But she

56

sat down on one of the chairs as if the offer of tea had only been a gesture.

'I'm very sorry about your son.' If only she really knew, thought Boyd. He began to sweat.

'You find it too hot in here? You're sweating.' The observation shocked him; for a minute he felt as if Rila Kovak could see into his very soul.

'I'm fine. It's cold outside.'

'I'm used to that.'

'What kind of heating do you have in here?' Now he sounded like a parish worker.

'The electric fire. Nothing else.'

'That's not very adequate.' He tried again. 'I'm very sorry about your son.'

'He should be in here. With me. Not in a funeral place.'

'I understand that.' Boyd knew exactly what she felt.

'But I was told the room is not suitable for a corpse, so I make myself unpopular by spending a lot of time at the funeral place. A man waits outside. The director I think. He is coughing. He is impatient for me to go. But I don't.'

'Where will Stefan be buried?'

'He is to be cremated. The priest tells me there is no room in the graveyard.' She paused. 'I would like to take him home, but that is not possible. I can't go back.'

'This is terrible.'

'Why should you care?'

Boyd tried to meet her eyes.

'None of us are welcome here,' Rila Kovac said bitterly. 'Stefan's death just means one less to house.' Oddly, she smiled for the first time and the smile changed her face. She was also smiling with her eyes – unlike her son's photograph. 'Are you English?'

'Yes,' said Boyd.

'And what do you think about us? About asylum seekers?'

'You are in a very difficult position.'

57

'We are a burden. The town is already a slum.'
'And has been for years. Long before you came.'
'We don't make it any more attractive.'
'You've got to live somewhere while you're waiting.'
'We'll be waiting for the rest of our lives.'
'Would you like a representative of Seekers to be present at the funeral?'
'What for?'
'As a mark of respect.'
She shrugged and didn't answer. 'You say you came to give me money. How much?'
'Sixty-five pounds.'
'OK. I'll take it.' She paused. 'This comes from the State?'
'From the funds of Seekers.'
'You mean – people collect for us?'
'We've been given some grant money.'
'For me?'
'Asylum seekers in general.'
'When can I have the money?'
'You just have to sign this form,' he said, passing it to her.
'Is the money for the funeral?'
'It's for your personal use.'
'Would you like a glass of brandy?'
Boyd looked surprised. 'Did you bring a bottle over with you?'
'I stole it from Tesco's.'
Boyd said nothing, almost amused by her directness.
'You don't like me doing that?'
'It's dangerous.'
'The drink?'
'The stealing.'
They both laughed gently and ruefully.
'I'm going to have one. Will you join me?'
Boyd shook his head.
She took out a quarter-full bottle of brandy from a

cupboard and poured a generous quantity into a cup. Then she took a long swig.

'I'll sign the form.'

Boyd got up and stood behind her chair to show Rila where to sign. But as she passed the document back, she took his hand and began to cry. The suddenness of the tears unnerved him.

'What will I do without him?'

'It's dreadful for you.'

'I'm empty.'

'I understand.'

'I want someone to help me.'

'That's why I'm here.'

'I need comfort.'

Boyd suddenly realized that she was offering him sex. Sex with her son's killer.

'I have to go now.' He had to leave. He couldn't take any more of the grief he had caused her.

'So no money?' Her voice was bitter.

'Of course you'll have the money.'

'I steal. That's not helpful to the reputation of the asylum seekers. You will think of us as a bad lot.'

Boyd went to the door. 'I'm very sorry.'

She didn't look up.

Harry Day stood on the snow-covered pebbles of the Seagate beach. It was high tide and there was ice in the heaving waves.

This was Seagate at its best, he thought, staring out at the lumpy sea, wondering if the Ice Breaker Club would really have to live up to its name when its members plunged into the waves tomorrow morning. All winter he, Jack King, Carl Bennett and half a dozen other local men had taken an early morning dip in the freezing sea and had enjoyed the invigorating experience. But tonight he was tired and drained, over-burdened by the knowledge that hung like a weight round his neck. He knew he should speak to someone, but he didn't want to do it without the agreement of the others. The three of them would have to meet again and try to make up their minds – unlike the last time.

Then he swung round in the darkness, conscious of someone's presence.

'I didn't see you there,' he said.

'I'm sorry.'

'I thought I was alone.'

'Yes.'

'Did you want to speak to me?'

'I saw you on the beach. I thought it might be the right time.'

'For what?' asked Harry Day.

Chapter Seven

Boyd was so exhausted that he slept dreamlessly until eight when his mobile rang. For a confused moment he thought Rila had got hold of his number. But the voice was Creighton's.

'There's been a development,' he said. 'Are you alone?'

'Yes.'

'You met Harry Day?'

'Yes.'

'What did you make of him?'

'He seemed to be very perceptive.'

'He won't be any longer. He's dead.'

Boyd was appalled. Events were running out of control – events that maybe he, personally, should have controlled. He was conscious of sudden failure, of not being sufficiently committed to his identity.

'How?'

'His body was washed up on the beach this morning.'

'Cause of death?'

'How about drowning?' asked Creighton testily. 'But we're not sure about that,' he admitted. 'There's a wound on his head, although it could have been caused by drifting into the girders of the pier. The tide was right for that. Did you know he was a member of the Ice Breakers – a winter swimming club?'

'I hadn't got that far.'

'The police called me.'

'I should have been more in the thick of things.'

'You don't seem to have found your feet yet.' Creighton sounded unusually impatient.

'What do you want me to do?'

'Go in to the office as usual. Take it from there.'

'Is there anything else you can tell me? Like the other members of this club?' Boyd suddenly focused. 'You mean they were swimming in this weather?' He got up and pulled the curtains back. No more snow had fallen, but the ground was still freezing hard.

'Day had been in the water for some time. We think he died last night. Can't be sure, though. There are two other members of the Ice Breakers you must see. Jack King, a local businessman, and Carl Bennett, a journalist on the *Seagate Observer*.'

'Could Day's death have been an accident?'

'Yes.'

'But you don't think it was.'

'It doesn't feel like an accident.'

Patronizing bastard, thought Boyd. Creighton knew perfectly well that any insider had to work his way into the labyrinth. Early results were unlikely.

'I went to see Rila Kovac – the mother of the –'

'I know who she is.' Creighton didn't sound impressed. 'What the hell did you do that for?'

'I was asked to see her by Seekers. As a first job.'

'The deep end?'

'I managed all right. They had a little money to give her.'

'She accepted?'

'Yes.'

'Did you do the religious stuff?'

'I was asked not to.'

'I don't think that should have been part of your new identity. I'm sorry about that.'

Boyd felt a sense of shock. Creighton never apologized. This was a first.

'What shall I do?'

'Tone it down. Tell me something – I get the impression that there's a problem with Rick James.'

'What kind of problem?'

'That you're finding it difficult to draw on his mantle. Am I right?'

'Yes.'

'After the boy.'

'Yes.'

'Are you going to the funeral?'

'Probably with Hanley.'

'That would be the correct thing to do.'

'Yes.'

'But deeply painful. I'm very sorry.'

'I don't want to talk about it. I need to get into James.'

'I hope so.' Creighton paused and then asked, 'Do the right people know you're available?'

'I've yet to find out. There's this newly formed central council amongst the asylum seekers.'

'Who are they?'

'Mile Kropitz from Albania, Edina Milstein from Lubic, Fitim Kadric from Bosnia and Josif Genzo from Kosovo. They've all been in Seagate for some time, inhabit the Grand and are said to be influential.'

'Know anything about them?'

'According to Hanley, Kropitz was a farmer, Kadric an Orthodox priest and Genzo an ex-army officer. He didn't seem to know anything about Milstein.'

'And Hanley?'

'As you know, he's the only employed member of Seekers and any likeness to a retired bank manager is entirely coincidental. I've only your word to go on that he's a police informer and maybe some sort of double agent.'

'Don't underestimate him.'

'No?'

'Local intelligence doesn't.'

'*Is* there any local intelligence?'

'Come on, Danny.'

Boyd frowned. 'You think I'll be approached as a potential recruit. But what kind of potential recruit?'

'We don't know yet. But I'm sure Hanley does.'

'How?'

'He's been given a connection. Hasn't he opened up?'

'Not so you'd notice,' said Boyd drily. 'Who told him?'

'Faraday.'

'So if he's the double agent you think he is, that bank raid was unnecessary,' said Boyd angrily.

Creighton didn't reply.

'I killed the boy for nothing.' Boyd snapped off the mobile and stared out at the grey ice. Suddenly he felt the bump as the green van drove over Stefan Kovac.

Hanley looked shocked and exhausted when Boyd arrived at the Seekers office.

'Have you heard what's happened?' Hanley asked.

'No.'

'Day's drowned. He was washed up on the beach this morning. I would have thought it was all over the local grapevine.'

Boyd hoped his shocked expression was adequate. 'I'm not on the local grapevine yet.'

'It's terrible. Day has always supported us to the hilt. We'll miss him dreadfully.'

When are you going to come clean and contact me? wondered Boyd. Is this the time? Or do you need to test me out some more? He heard Creighton's voice in his mind. '*He's been given a connection.*' He certainly didn't show any sign of it.

'Was his death an accident?' Boyd asked.

'I don't think so.'

'Why not?'

'Day was a magnificent swimmer. He was in the Ice Breakers – the winter swimming club.'

'You mean they swim in these conditions?'

'It would take a lot to stop them.'

'What time was he found?'

'They usually swim at about eight in the morning.'

'And –'

'Day's body was found well before eight. The others hadn't even turned up.' He broke off as Boyd interrupted.

'Did they always go together?'

'Yes. But I've been in touch with the police. Faraday told me the pathologist says Day's body had been in the water for a few hours. Maybe since last night. They'll know for sure soon.' Hanley turned to the kettle and filled a teapot. He poured out a cup for himself and offered Boyd one which he refused. 'The local radio station's just given out that he was fully dressed.'

'So he didn't just go for a swim.'

They gazed at each other.

'I'm very sorry. He seemed a good man.'

'He was.'

'And Seekers?'

'Business as usual.' Hanley paused, wrenching himself away from the tragedy. 'How did you get on with Mrs Kovac?' he asked.

'She's signed the form. I've got it here.' Boyd put the paper on Hanley's desk and they both looked at it without speaking. Hanley smoothed the form out and Boyd saw that his hands were trembling. 'This must have come as the most dreadful shock.' Boyd winced at the banal words.

Hanley looked impatient. 'The best thing I can do for Harry Day is to carry on.' He was almost dismissive.

'Of course.'

'How was Mrs Kovac?'

'In very bad shape.'

'An unnecessary tragedy,' said Hanley, and Boyd wondered if this was the moment he'd been waiting for. 'But

65

the asylum seekers are desperate for money,' he added flatly.

'Do you think they could have had anything to do with Day's death?'

'Day was trying to *help* them.' Hanley's voice shook, but he looked at Boyd searchingly.

'Obviously he was,' said Boyd quickly. 'But he said himself that he felt some of them were being recruited by criminals. Do you think he was on to anything specific?'

'I don't know.' Hanley looked very worried.

'I can imagine some kind of volatile situation could have been building up,' Boyd probed, but Hanley refused to be drawn.

'So was Rila Kovac happy to have the money?' he asked.

'Happy in no way describes her. She's desperate and made no secret of the fact that she steals brandy.'

'She may have been doing that before her son was killed. But their lives are intolerable. I told you – they all need a lot of support and encouragement.'

'I certainly didn't lecture her. She offered me a drink. Naturally I refused,' he added hastily.

There was a long silence.

'Do you have another job for me?'

Hanley nodded, as if glad to be prompted. 'Yes. There's a meeting of the central council today, in the Grand Hotel at noon. Kropitz, Milstein, Kadric and Genzo. Usually I go, but in the circumstances perhaps you wouldn't mind standing in for me.'

'They're not going to like that much, are they?'

'That's their problem,' said Hanley brusquely.

The sun was a hard, bright orange orb in a cold cobalt blue sky. There was no wind, but the heat wasn't strong enough to even begin to melt the impacted snow.

In the bright hostile light the Grand seemed even more shabby than before, window frames peeling and rust running in gouts from the drainpipes on to the scarred frontage.

Maybe if he handled this meeting with the asylum seekers well, Hanley would have enough confidence to draw him in. But the meeting didn't sound easy to handle at all and Boyd felt increasingly anxious as he entered the run-down foyer.

A tall woman, dressed in faded jeans and a long coat, was heading towards a corridor at the back and Boyd saw there was an arrow on the wall and a faded sign which read TO THE BALLROOM.

'Excuse me,' said Boyd, and she turned.

'What is it?' The woman had short, raggedly cut black hair and her long narrow face was sallow, but she was imperious and the bored glance she darted at Boyd was almost arrogant.

'I've come for the meeting. The meeting of the central council.'

'You?'

'Yes. My boss – Mr Hanley – usually attends, I believe.'

'And why is he not coming today?'

'Our president drowned. Hadn't you heard? It's all over town.'

'Yes,' she replied abruptly. 'I had heard.' She offered no commiseration. 'You'd better come with me then.'

'Thank you.'

She walked briskly ahead of him, carrying a super-market bag as if it was a dispatch box.

'I didn't catch your name,' said Boyd.

'I didn't give it to you.'

The ballroom smelt of Jeyes Fluid. Once the huge space must have been imposing, but now the paintwork was faded and the ceiling covered in damp patches. There were a few tables and chairs dotted around the floor, one still surreally covered with a dirty white cloth on which rested a single wineglass. Scaffold poles were stacked at one end of the room and the semicircular bar was dirty and stained.

The other members of the council were already seated round a table on the stage, gazing down with curiosity at the late arrivals.

'We have a visitor from Seekers.'

'Where's Mr Hanley?' The man was overweight, dressed in a heavy suit with an open-neck shirt.

'He's otherwise engaged.'

'Because of Day's death?'

'Yes,' said Boyd. 'I'm a new member of staff at Seekers and Mr Hanley hoped that you would allow me to sit in.'

'It isn't a regular occurrence,' said the man. 'Mr Hanley only came occasionally, and at our invitation.'

'I'm sorry.' Boyd knew he would have to fight to stay. Why hadn't Hanley briefed him better than this? He felt a surge of resentment.

'I hear you visited Stefan's mother.'

'Yes.'

'She was very pleased. I didn't realize your charity offered money. Soon there will be bees around your honeypot.'

'We don't have much of a honeypot,' said Boyd defensively.

The big man stood up with some effort and said, 'You'd better stay. Bring up a chair and join us. I'm Mile Kropitz, and the lady is Edina Milstein. To my right is Josif Genzo.' Genzo was tall and looked in good physical shape, with a shaved head and rigid lines at the sides of his mouth. 'And on my left is Fitim Kadric.' A small rather fussy-looking man nodded curtly at Boyd. He wore glasses on the bridge of his nose and his hair was swept back from a broad brow.

Boyd clumsily picked up a chair and followed Edina Milstein up on to the stage. He placed his chair hesitantly, some way from the others.

'My name is Rick James and, as I said, I've just joined Seekers.'

'You won't find many other members of staff besides Mr

Hanley,' replied Mile who seemed to be the self-appointed spokesman.

'I realize the job is very difficult.' Boyd made himself sound rueful.

'We are not a popular cause,' said Fitim. 'In fact we are the least popular cause you can imagine.'

'How long have you all been in this country?'

'A couple of years,' said Josif. 'We are experts at patience.'

'How long can you continue to be patient?' asked Boyd hesitantly.

'There is no way any of us can go back.'

'I'm sorry,' said Boyd, turning to the others. 'I am asking too many questions.'

None of them met his gaze.

Mile said, 'We must proceed with our meeting.' He paused. 'I regard you as an impartial observer. As we do for Mr Hanley – we shall speak in English.'

'Thank you very much.'

'It is probably for the best. We all come from different countries. At least they are different countries now.' He paused and then said, 'We are expecting a visitor.' He paused again. 'Roma Lorta.'

'He is a rather controversial figure,' said Fitim.

Boyd said nothing.

'You know of him?' demanded Edina, as if she was hoping to expose Boyd's ignorance.

'Yes, but I can't remember –'

Josif interrupted irritably, 'Lorta is the exiled President of Lubic – the Balkan state that has once again plunged into ethnic cleansing. The British and US governments want to reinstate him.'

'So, he is to come to Seagate.'

'And Margate and Ramsgate and Hastings and Great Yarmouth – all the places where the asylum seekers have been placed.' Edina spoke bitterly. 'DSS by the cold seaside. What could be nicer? We intend to show Lorta the terrible conditions under which we live. He is a strong man – a strong character. He could not only unite his own country – my country – but bring the plight of all the asylum seekers to the attention of the British public. We see him as a potential ambassador – and we need someone who can influence the British government. We can't go on under these conditions.' She spoke as if she had made the speech many times. There was a boredom in her – more than a boredom. A bored anger.

'Where will Lorta speak?' asked Boyd.

'This ballroom. The state of the place is a good example of the overall conditions.'

'Who owns the Grand?'

'A property company,' said Fitim Kadric. 'They were going to convert the hotel into an apartment block. But now they think, why spend the money doing that when the British government will pay for so many of us to occupy a condemned building?'

'*Is* it condemned?' asked Boyd.

'It *should* be condemned,' said Josif.

'And you four all live here?'

They nodded.

'There is so little Seekers can do in the short term,' said Boyd guardedly.

'Don't let Mr Hanley hear you say that.' Edina smiled for the first time. 'To him, Seekers is a lobby group. But no one listens to him. Not the government and not the local authority. I'd never say this to him, but Seekers is just – what do you say? – a tinpot little organization.'

Boyd shrugged. 'You may be right. But he does his best – and so did Day – and then there's Hilary Browning.' He tried to sound hopeful.

'You can't be paid much.' Edina was gazing at him, making eye contact at last.

'Not a lot.'

'So why do you do the job?' asked Josif.

'I need to straighten myself out.' They were all gazing at him with greater interest. 'I was in prison,' Boyd added, and looked away.

'What was the charge?' asked Fitim.

'Fraud.'

'What kind of fraud?'

'Credit cards. I got a five-year sentence and I did three – released early for good behaviour. As a result I want to do something rather more worthwhile with my life – or does that sound too pious?'

'So you came to the end of the line,' said Edina. 'Isn't that what Seagate is best known for – the town at the end of the line?'

Boyd nodded.

'Do you have other motives?' asked Edina.

'Yes. I'm a Christian now.'

'Born-again?' Josif seemed amused.

'Put it like this – I want to lead a Christian life, but I wouldn't want to impose it on others.'

'You don't evangelize?'

'Definitely not.'

'The majority of us are Muslim,' said Mile Kropitz.

'And I'm Catholic,' contributed Edina. 'But that makes no difference and we're straying from the agenda.'

'That was my fault,' said Boyd.

'I do hope you're not one of those people who belittle themselves to make an impression,' said Edina sharply.

Boyd smiled. 'I don't think so.'

'The point is,' said Mile, 'we want to make sure Lorta's visit goes smoothly – but gets as much media coverage as possible. And that's not easy to achieve.'

'What are you expecting?' asked Boyd. 'Some kind of disruption?'

'There could be.'

'Who from?'

'Some asylum seekers dislike Lorta intensely – and dislike is a mild word.'

'Why?'

'They think Lorta is for his own Muslim population. But there are others – in his country and here – that are not his own people.'

71

'You mean there could be more ethnic cleansing –'

'He won't do that,' said Edina. 'But, as I say, some people feel that Lorta will keep his own people around him and the rest will be regarded as second-class citizens.' She paused. 'I don't believe that myself.'

'You left Lubic because you were a victim of ethnic cleansing? Have you lost your family?' Boyd risked a little more probing. He didn't want them to think he was only a humble or idealistic do-gooder.

'Yes,' said Edina baldly and there was an awkward silence.

'Are you worried that there could be some kind of threat to Lorta while he's here?' Boyd turned to Fitim Kadric.

'There is considerable threat to him wherever there are asylum seekers.'

'The police will be taking precautions.'

'Of course. But we are concerned they won't take enough. There is a very real threat of assassination and that's why we're meeting today.' Kadric paused, looking worried. 'We would ask you not to pass on any details of our conversation.'

'Even to Hanley?'

'Especially Mr Hanley.'

Boyd felt a stab of surprise. 'Why's that?'

'We don't trust him,' said Edina.

'For any particular reason?'

'He reports everything back to his management committee.'

And to the police, thought Boyd, who are a rather more powerful form of management committee.

'Couldn't that be helpful in creating more security?' Josif intervened.

'I just think it reflects badly on asylum seekers everywhere,' said Edina. 'We don't have a very good reputation in this country. Assassination attempts – or even the possibility of them – don't help to improve that reputation.'

'Of course not.' Boyd could see he would have to take

the conversation a step further. 'And of course the every-day exterior of Seagate has just been severely ruffled.'

'I don't understand what you mean,' said Edina.

'Some bad things have happened,' Boyd said quietly.

'You mean the bank raid?'

'And the drowning of Harry Day.'

'Surely that was an accident?'

Boyd wondered if he was moving too fast. Then he knew he couldn't miss the opportunity.

'Hanley has some doubts about that.'

'Why? He was a cold sea swimmer. God knows, nothing would tempt me to punish myself like that,' said Josif.

'Apparently he enjoyed it. But the police think he was in the water at the wrong time, that he didn't just go for a swim after all.'

'Could the police be wrong?' asked Fitim.

'Quite possibly. But suppose – just suppose – they're not.'

'Are you saying that the killing of Stefan and the drowning of this man Day could be linked?'

'All I'm saying is that I've been told there's been a considerable petty crime wave in Seagate recently.' Boyd tried to sound uncertain. 'But nothing on this scale.'

'People blame what you call a petty crime wave on us – the asylum seekers.' Edina sounded hostile. 'But the unemployment rate, for your own people, is incredibly high.'

'Asylum seekers may commit crimes too,' said Josif. 'It's just that I don't see why we should be blamed for every one of them.'

'Is that what the police do?'

'It's what everyone does.'

'You feel you're often discriminated against?'

'Don't be foolish, Mr James,' snapped Edina. 'We are *always* discriminated against.'

'Let me get this right.' Boyd decided to step up the pressure. 'You are being discriminated against; no asylum seeker is a criminal.'

'Rubbish.' Edina was angry. 'Of course there are some. But we're not the only ones.'

'Your English is very good,' said Boyd, deliberately trying to lighten the atmosphere. 'That is a favourite expression of ours – "We're not the only ones."'

She had the grace to laugh and the others smiled. There was a definite relaxing of tension and Boyd immediately capitalized on it in an attempt to gain their confidence. 'All I'm suggesting is that there's an escalating crime wave in Seagate, and now a bank raid. Let's leave Day out of it for the moment. Couldn't there be any link between the criminal underworld in the town and a group of asylum seekers?'

'Why should there be?'

'An assassination needs setting up. It's not a job for amateurs.'

'So you believe that there is some kind of link,' said Josif, 'between the criminal element in Seagate and the criminal element amongst the asylum seekers.'

'There might be.'

'Why the bank raid?'

'Assassinations have to be funded.'

'Do you suppose Day's death is part of this?' Josif looked very worried.

'I've no idea.' Boyd wanted to pull back now. 'I can't work that out. All I'm saying is that Roma Lorta is coming to Seagate and already things have started to happen.'

'They could be completely unconnected,' said Mile Kropitz.

'Of course.'

'Why did you really join Seekers, Mr James?' asked Edina suddenly, and for a terrible moment Boyd thought he had given himself away.

'I wanted to do a job I could get my teeth into,' he said quickly. 'In other words I wanted a challenge. This is my chance to turn my life around, to get a grip on myself. Does that make any sense?'

'Please don't think us so naive, Mr James,' said Josif

sceptically. 'You have such altruistic motives that they are virtually unbelievable.'

'No one could be so good,' said Edina. 'So blindingly, absolutely good.'

'I'm not good, but I've lost everything – like you have. That's why I was attracted to Seekers in the first place,' Boyd continued firmly, knowing that he had failed to convince them and would have to release all his shot and shell. 'My parents are dead. My wife and children have deserted me. I'm alone. I feel like an asylum seeker myself. All I know is that I stand alone and want to work with those who stand alone as well.'

It was a pretty little speech and sounded almost acceptable. On another level, however, it was bitterly true as far as Boyd himself was concerned, and he could feel his so far shaky grip on Rick James's identity beginning to tighten. To his surprise his diatribe seemed to reach Milstein, Kadric, Kropitz and Genzo, and Boyd was pleased that he had given them at least a semblance of the truth.

'We appreciate your honesty,' said Josif. 'And I can see and understand the link between us. We'll take seriously what you say about the criminal activity and its possible link to the current situation.'

'There's only one problem,' said Edina.

'What's that?' asked Boyd awkwardly.

'We are not undercover agents.'

Boyd felt a surge of panic and struggled to suppress it. Was she playing with him in some way?

'We can't infiltrate our own people. There are many groups here, many different problems. That's why Lorta's life could be in danger when he comes.'

'Do you have a police contact?' Boyd asked.

'DI Faraday. We've met with him several times.'

'And expressed your fears?'

'Yes.'

'Then there's nothing else you can do.'

There was a pause and then Edina Milstein said quietly,

'I must say I find your commitment impressive, Mr James. I can't say the same for Mr Hanley.'

'Wait a minute.' Kadric interrupted Milstein anxiously. 'This is not a case for comparison.'

'Isn't it?' Milstein seemed surprised. 'Personally, I find Mr Hanley rather ineffective.' She turned back to Boyd. 'Do you understand?'

'No,' replied Boyd unhelpfully. 'Tell me what you really mean.'

'Of course he's there on his own, deserted by staff and volunteers. But he doesn't seem concerned. It's almost as if he's waiting for something to happen.'

'He gave me money for Rila Kovac.'

'So?'

'At least he can be practical. *We* can be practical.' Boyd didn't want to go too far in protecting Hanley. Abruptly he changed the subject. 'Do you know when Lorta is scheduled to arrive?' he asked.

'On Saturday.'

'That doesn't give you much time to check things out.'

'Exactly.'

There was a long silence and Boyd realized they were hoping he would leave. He got up and shook hands with them all, wondering what they would say about him when he had gone.

As he went down the steps of the stage, Edina Milstein suddenly called after him, 'The boy's funeral is this afternoon.'

Chapter Eight

Boyd lay on his bed, exhausted by the morning's meeting. Slowly he drifted off to sleep and dreamt that he was naked and chasing a balloon over the shingle beach. Eventually the balloon came to rest on one of the seaweed-hung girders beneath the pier. Boyd plunged into water that was as heavy as lead. He waded towards the balloon which, caught in a sudden breeze, wafted away from the pier. Boyd could just make out a name. Richard James.

His mobile rang and he woke, muzzily fumbling in his pocket.

'Mr James?'

'Yes.'

'This is DI Faraday. I hope you don't mind me calling you on your mobile.'

'Go ahead.'

'I reckon it's safer to contact you this way. I'm in touch with Mr Creighton, of course. Do you want to tell me how you are getting on – or isn't this a good moment?'

'It's OK. Apparently Lorta arrives on Saturday.'

'Yes. I've drafted in extra men, but I'm not expecting too much trouble.'

'You aren't expecting an assassination attempt –'

'Good God, no! Lorta's a moderate. One of the old brigade like Tito. The general belief is that he can draw the country together and stabilize it too. He has a strong personality and a good following.'

'Has he done the rounds of asylum seekers before?'

'No.' There was a long pause. 'Do I sense that you feel we're being complacent?'

'I don't know. I've just been to a meeting of this newly formed central council. They seem to be worried.'

'We're taking every possible precaution.'

'I'm sure you are,' said Boyd smoothly. 'I take it you're talking about Kropitz, Milstein, Kadric and Genzo?'

'Yes.'

'What were your impressions of them?'

'They're decent people as far as I could tell.' Boyd paused. 'Can you fill me in on Hanley?'

'What about him?'

'Is he a police informer?'

'I occasionally have information from him about the asylum-seeker community.' Faraday sounded vague.

'You can tell me.' Boyd paused. 'You *should* tell me.'

'It's better you don't know.'

'I need to know,' Boyd insisted.

Faraday sighed. 'OK,' he said reluctantly. 'We planted Hanley. I didn't think there was any reason for you to know that.'

'I understand.' Boyd wanted to encourage him. 'What's Hanley's assignment?'

'He was a police informer in Bradford. He's on his own, no attachments. He's worked in charities before.'

'Is he gay?'

'I suspect he keeps all that in the closet. His last job was in a charity representing animal rights. We like to get him inside communities.'

'Just like me,' said Boyd. 'Pity I didn't know that before.'

'My opinion is that the less you know the better you'll get on. Creighton believes that too.'

Boyd knew he did. 'How many other informers have you got out there? A battalion or two?'

Faraday didn't reply. Then he said, 'As an undercover officer, you're proactive. You're not an informer. Hanley's job is to keep an ear to the ground. Yours is to penetrate.'

'But wouldn't you be better off tapping an asylum seeker?'

'I'm not sure who I can trust in that quarter. There's a lot of manipulation. I'd rather go for Hanley, at least for the moment. He's giving us a pretty accurate picture of what's going on.'

'And the bank raid?'

'He hasn't made any reference to it.'

There was another silence.

'I'm very sorry about the boy.' Faraday sounded genuine. 'A horrible accident.'

Boyd didn't want to reply. 'Do you think I could still be approached?'

'That was the plan.'

'I hope to God it hasn't misfired, bearing in mind the aftermath.'

'I think you could still be approached,' said Faraday.

'About killing Lorta?'

'That could be a possibility.'

'How useful has Hanley been?'

'So far he's given us information about who's doing what to whom and which of the asylum seekers are almost certainly engaged in criminal activities.'

'I got the impression from Creighton that *Hanley* might approach me.'

'We don't know for sure if he's working for anyone else.' Faraday dropped the bombshell with some satisfaction.

'But you think he is?'

'He's a clever guy, but the information he's giving us is still valuable. I don't want to stop that. Hanley believes you're an efficient, professional criminal, in the right place and at the right time. You've been effectively planted. Let's see what he does next.'

Before going to the funeral, Boyd went into the Seekers

office and gave Hanley an edited version of what had happened at the meeting. He seemed pleased.

Boyd wore a dark suit he had had for many years and a pale tie. He wondered if he was correctly dressed.

'You seem to have got on well with the council.'

'I hope so.'

'Edina Milstein phoned me. She was full of praise. But how did *you* assess the situation?'

Boyd sensed that Hanley was infinitely more astute than the middle-aged nondescript image he presented.

'The community here seems very despondent,' said Boyd. 'The waiting game is beginning to tell. Poverty and despair undermine anyone.'

'And what do they reckon about Lorta?'

'He could well be at risk.'

There was a pause.

'How long have you been working for Seekers?' asked Boyd casually.

'A year or so. It's been uphill work.'

Their eyes met and Boyd mentally urged Hanley to make a breakthrough, to contact him now. But maybe he wasn't ready yet, and if Hanley wasn't ready there had to be a reason. Boyd guessed he still didn't know whether he could be trusted.

'I'm going to the funeral now,' said Boyd. 'Is there anything you would like me to do afterwards?'

'Do you have plans?' asked Hanley.

'I was going to look up Stefan's mother again. See how she's getting on.'

'It might be better if you didn't do that.'

Boyd gave him a surprised look. 'Why not?' He was genuinely puzzled.

'She is vulnerable.'

'You mean I could become too involved with her?'

'Something like that. I hope I haven't offended you.'

'No.' Boyd was slightly thrown. Clearly he still hadn't got Hanley's measure, but he was becoming increasingly convinced that Faraday was right and that under Hanley's bland exterior there was the sharpest of minds.

As they stood in the crematorium chapel, Father Tristan walked slowly up the aisle, followed by the coffin which was carried by four asylum seekers, young men in their early twenties.

Rila Kovac was in the front pew with Edina Milstein as the coffin was placed on a plinth in front of some dark blue curtains – the beginning of the production line to the flames. The chapel was tightly packed with asylum seekers. A pity Hanley hadn't put in a showing, thought Boyd. He felt self-conscious amongst the silent crowd, aware that his suit and ill-matching tie made him closely resemble an undertaker.

The electric organ was playing 'Abide With Me' as Father Tristan placed a hand on the coffin.

'This innocent child was robbed of his life,' he said. 'The tragedy is very great for Rila Kovac. Stefan was her only child, her only relative. Whoever killed him will have Stefan's death on his conscience for the rest of his life. May he be forgiven.'

The chapel, even in the freezing conditions, was so hot that Boyd began to sweat, but something cold crawled into the pit of his stomach.

As Father Tristan began to conduct the service, many of the asylum seekers started to weep and Boyd had never felt so vulnerable in his life. He remembered a scene in Northern Ireland, when a couple of British soldiers had been captured by the mob and beaten to death. He also recalled the grim photograph of a priest kneeling by a badly wounded soldier and giving him the last rites.

Suppose someone here in the chapel knew what he had done? Would he be torn apart by the crowd? The sweat was trickling into his eyes and Boyd rubbed it away. He felt completely exposed and had a wild urge to walk up to the coffin and stand by Father Tristan, admitting to what he had done.

'*I ran him over,*' said a voice in his mind. '*Listen to me. I ran him over. I killed Stefan.*'

Boyd's throat was dry, so dry he could barely croak out the responses, and he made no attempt to join in the singing.

'There is a green hill far away,
Without a city wall,
Where the dear Lord was crucified,
Who died to save us all . . .'

Boyd gazed around him discreetly, wondering who would understand the words of such an English hymn. Few were singing and only Father Tristan's voice could be heard, a strong baritone that soared around the functional chapel.

This is my crucifixion, thought Boyd. He had never felt so isolated, never so damned in his own eyes. Years ago he had killed his entire family. Now he had killed again. No wonder he had such difficulty in playing the role of Rick James.

'The Lord is my shepherd, I shall not want,' began Father Tristan. 'He maketh me to lie down in green pastures. He leadeth me beside the still waters . . .'

Green again, thought Boyd. But then the Balkans were green, so perhaps the words weren't so alien after all. Now tears were pouring down Boyd's cheeks and he couldn't control them. Maybe that was for the best.

Chapter Nine

Edina Milstein had Rila Kovac on her arm when Boyd arrived in the snow-covered garden of the crematorium. Little groups of asylum seekers were shivering and then Boyd saw a well-built broad-shouldered man with just the hint of a paunch walking towards him. He was dressed in a rather stylish Italian suit with button-down collar and tie under a dark overcoat.

Catching Boyd's eye, the man paused and then walked over to Father Tristan, as if he had suddenly thought better of approaching him. Instantly Boyd was sure he must be Faraday.

'I'll kill him. If I ever meet him, I'll kill him,' Rila was sobbing.

'I'm so very sorry.' Boyd looked at the ground, unable to meet the eyes of either woman.

Edina Milstein gave him an impatient glance.

'I need to take her home now,' she said.

'Take me home?' snarled Rila Kovac. 'Where the fucking hell is home?' She pulled out her bottle of brandy just as Father Tristan came up. They looked at each other uneasily.

'Do you know where Edina Milstein lives?' Boyd had wandered the icy streets of Seagate after he left the funeral. But as darkness fell he had made his way back to the Grand.

The man was wearing a long overcoat and dark glasses and Boyd took a few minutes to recognize Fitim Kadric. 'What is that English expression? You are haunting the place, Mr James.'

'I wanted to ask her a few more questions about the plight of an asylum seeker.'

'Weren't you briefed by Hanley?'

'Of course. But there's nothing like –'

'The real thing,' Kadric finished for him. 'Do you want to talk to me?'

'If you're available.' Boyd forced himself to sound grateful.

'But I don't have long legs and a nice arse.'

'No. I don't think you do.' Boyd laughed and then wondered if he was being a little too tolerant for a religious man. 'I just want to talk to Edina, that's all.'

Kadric had the grace to look a little awkward. 'She's up on the second floor. Number seventeen. And I know she's in.'

'Thanks.' Boyd began to stride up the stairs, all too conscious that Kadric was watching him curiously.

Boyd knocked on her door and waited for some time before he saw Edina's eyes watching him through the security panel. Then the door was slowly but purposefully opened.

'Good heavens, Mr James.' The way she spoke made him smile. 'What's the joke?' Edina asked.

'You certainly have plenty of English expressions.'

'I pick them up.'

'Do you mind if I come in and ask you a few questions?'

'What about?'

'The situation amongst the asylum seekers in Seagate. But I can go and ask someone else if –'

'No. Come in.' Edina relented. 'You'll be a distraction.'

Boyd followed her into a much larger space than he had

expected – a big central room with a small bathroom and kitchen. While the furniture was shabby – probably remnants of the original Grand Hotel stock – there was a large modern television and the carpet was spotless.

Edina sat down on a sofa covered by a throw and Boyd sat opposite her on a hard chair. He was beginning to wonder if the visit had been a good idea.

'What do you want to ask me?'

'I was very conscious at that meeting of being the new boy and not knowing nearly as much as I should about asylum seekers.'

'I didn't mean to be off-putting.'

'Are you sure I'm not intruding? After the funeral and –'

'I'd tell you if you were.'

'Thanks.' Boyd cleared his throat. 'How long do you reckon you'll have to wait for British nationality?'

'Only a few more months, I hope. Surely it can't go on any longer . . .' She seemed immediately depressed, and then said, 'Do you have time to hear my story?'

'Of course. But I don't want to –'

'Please don't think me rude, but could you shut up for a moment? I haven't told my story in a long while. My friends – the other members of the central council – know every detail and I know every detail of theirs. We have too much time to kill and use it up by telling and retelling our life stories. The atmosphere in this small bleak town is so claustrophobic that it's as if we've been in prison together for a very long time – and to pass that time we've given each other our lives. In one way I feel so public that I can barely cope. There is nothing that Mile, Fitim and Josif or even Rila don't know about me – or I about them. We've all had tragedies – Rila most recently – but now we know them so well they lack reality. Do you know what I mean, Mr James?'

'Of course I do.'

'OK. Let me tell you my story then. Stop me if I go on too long.'

Boyd waited for her to begin.

Edina Milstein closed her eyes. 'I'm there now. Whenever I shut my eyes, I can see our house in a small village in the hills. Carna. Tiga and Kerno Tasam had lived next door to us all our lives. They are Muslims. We are Catholics. The children had grown up together. The Tasams' three sons and the Milsteins' two sons and a daughter. The daughter, of course, is me. I was brought up in what seemed like a male enclave. I was the youngest and worked in a small clothing factory in a nearby town. The boys were in professional jobs and had all gone; I was the only stay-at-home and that was because I dearly loved the place. There were mountains beyond and we were in the foothills. The air was fresh and my father, before he died, had a small farm which he sold to a family we knew well when he became ill.'

Edina paused. She had been looking in Boyd's direction, but he could see she was now staring straight through him. He felt empty and irrelevant.

'So there we were. A young woman in her mid-twenties and three old people. It was a bit like being trapped in time, but I was in love with the foothills, always have been, and I spent all my free time walking and re-exploring.

'This place, this dump – Seagate – is alive only with jealousy and frustration and the need to find any means of escape. There are drugs here and an awful lot of young people use them. Now this man Day has been murdered.'

Edina paused and then looked away, returning to the past. 'Nothing like that had reached Carna and although we'd sold the farm I was still able to wander round the fields safely. Ours was a tight community. If you had told me about ethnic cleansing, of neighbour turning against neighbour, I would have thought you were crazy.

'I wonder sometimes why I didn't yearn for the cities like the boys did. I went to English courses in the town, but I never stayed the night. I'd been born into a place I loved and at that time I didn't want anything else – not even a husband and babies. I suppose I thought they would come eventually. I wanted children. Why I loved my foothills – my place of birth – to such an extent I didn't know. My mother used to laugh at me but I knew she loved me deeply and was glad to keep me with her. To her I was a gift. My father, I know, had worried about me, and thought I was stagnating, but after he died there was no one to disturb the pattern, to criticize a way of life that held no ambition and consisted of living for the moment. And the moments didn't change. Until recently.

'I will always remember that day. The cleansing had begun in the cities and we were shocked and horrified, but not as afraid as you might think. Once again, in the foothills, the countryside seemed to be insulated against what was happening – even when it began to spread. I thought my world, my time capsule, was strong enough to keep the horrors out.

'Nothing seemed to change between us and our neighbours. The two houses were very near, along a road that was only used for farm traffic. It was rutted and wasn't a route anyone else would take. There wasn't even a signpost. We were in nowhere. I fancied that idea. We lived in nowhere until the day came.

'Please, Mr James, don't think of me as an innocent. I wasn't even a virgin because one of the boys next door had taken me. Nowadays, in this country, that taking would be called rape. But to me it was a natural event – as natural as the animals in the fields. Do you find me so very pathetic?'

'No,' said Boyd, and was surprised to find how touched he felt at her openness. 'I don't.'

'The day came,' she repeated. 'The only difference I saw at home since the cleansing in the towns was that the Tasams had become a little withdrawn. Tiga, the mother, well, she didn't come and see my mother any more. But we even accepted that. God knows, I was a fool being so blind, turning away from reality, hanging on to my little world, clutching it to my bosom so hard I couldn't see the danger coming.

'That day I'd just got back from work and had had a shower. Mother was in the kitchen, cooking our supper. I remember she was making a casserole. She was a fine cook and I always looked forward to our evening meal together when she would relate the tiny details of her day and I would relate the tiny details of mine.

'I'd put on a dressing gown. It was summer, bakingly hot, and I could smell the heat as I always could – a mixture of hay and dry earth.

'Then I heard a step outside and I looked out of the window and was surprised to see the Tasams standing in our garden. Kerno had something in a bag under his arm and Tiga was standing beside him, looking down at the ground in a dejected way, as if she had had bad news. For a moment I wondered about my brothers. Or their boys. Had there been an accident? I felt momentarily afraid as my mother took the casserole out of the oven and placed it carefully on the table. Then she went to get some cold water from the fridge.

'I gazed out of the window. My mother saw me and stared out too. What the hell was going on? Tiga and Kerno were still standing there.

'Slowly Tiga came to the door and knocked. My mother almost ran, she was so eager. "Maybe we can be good neighbours again. Maybe this is the way they are showing us. Maybe –" She plunged towards the door and pulled it open. "Tiga," she cried out, but I couldn't hear a reply.

'Then there was a strange sound – a kind of thump – and I wondered if, in her haste, my mother had fallen. I hurried to the door. Kerno was standing there with something in his hand while Tiga wept silently beside him. Then he pointed the gun at me.

'I looked down and saw my mother lying on the ground. She was on her back with her eyes staring up at the mountains. They didn't blink and she had her mouth open, her dentures slightly detached from her gums. There was a little round hole in her forehead.

'I plunged towards her and Kerno's shot must have gone wide. I heard the dull thud again as the bullet hit the lintel of the door. I screamed and went on screaming. I didn't think I was ever going to stop. I could see the foothills. There was a slight mist dispersing in the baking summer heat and I could hear the stream tinkling, the silence was so deep.

'It was the instinct of self-preservation that saved me. Before he could fire again I had turned round and run back into the house.

'By this time I was numb, but I still knew I had to get out of the way, get the hell out of Kerno's range. The fact that my mother was dead and that she'd been murdered hardly reached me at all. I wanted to live – to walk in the foothills amongst the sheep – and I was possessed by the most primitive need to survive.

'I ran into the kitchen while Kerno lumbered after me. He was a slow-moving man, crippled with arthritis, and it was this arthritis that was to give me the chance to escape.

'I pulled open the back door and slammed it shut behind me. I had to run, to put as much distance as I could between him and me. That was all I could think of. That was all that I *had* to think of and this single-mindedness saved me. Now I was running uphill, leaving the house on the ridge below me.

'Kerno came out and stood on the rising ground, the gun in his hand.

'Then I saw that he was holding his gun with two hands to steady his aim, but it was still unbelievable that I was his target. I didn't know whether to try and hide, to throw myself on the ground, or keep on running. My instinct was to keep on running and hope I was out of range. There was a thud and then another but I was still running and soon I reached the brow of the hill.

'Pausing for a moment I stared down at Kerno. He was

still alone in our back garden and I was alone up on the hill. Yet we seemed to gaze into each other's eyes uncomprehendingly, as if we could barely recognize we were on opposite sides and that Kerno, who had been like an uncle to me, was trying to kill me.

'Then the shock hit me that my mother was dead and that Kerno had killed her. I threw myself down on the grass and began to cry, burying my head in the long stems and amongst the flowers. She was dead. She was dead. I had to accept she was dead, but I couldn't. As to Kerno, all I do is to loathe him a little more each day. If I could kill him – I would do that.'

Edina began to sob. There were no tears that Boyd could see – only the hard dry sobs that continued, almost rhythmically, as if they would never end.

Boyd got up and went over to her, drawn by her pain, wanting to comfort Edina whose experiences had been so dreadful, so unforgettable that she had needed a complete stranger as a sounding board.

'I'm sorry,' she said, pushing Boyd away when he put a hand on her shoulder. He stepped back respectfully, knowing even this sign of compassion was a mistake, and returned to his chair while Edina got up and went into the bathroom. He waited, not sure whether he should go or stay. Then she returned to the sofa and sat composedly, hands in her lap, as if she had just been confessing to a priest and was waiting for him to speak, to give her absolution.

'Thank you for telling me,' he said.

'I needed to.'

'Because everyone knows the story?'

'They've not been allowed to escape.' She smiled. 'Would you like some tea?'

'If you want me to stay.'

'Yes. I would like you to stay for a while.'

She got up and went into the kitchen.

Boyd stared down at the spotless carpet, knowing

instinctively that keeping the carpet clean was Edina's way of keeping sane.

She brought the tea in and put the tray on a small central table that neither of them could reach. Boyd looked at his watch. It was just after five.

'Are you in a hurry?'

'No.'

'You were looking at your watch.'

'I was surprised to find the time had gone so fast.'

They both stared at the tea and Edina laughed. 'Who is to serve who?'

Boyd jumped to his feet. 'Let me serve you.'

'I like it black with no sugar.'

'So do I.'

When they had their cups they looked at each other with sudden self-consciousness. 'I hope I didn't bore you,' she said.

'Bore me? Don't be so –'

'Stupid? I am very stupid about this story. I have to tell it again and again, and I'm very sorry. Perhaps Mr Day's widow will do the same. Do you know if he is married?'

'No. I wanted to hear your story. I feel privileged to have heard it. Can I ask you a question?'

'Of course.'

'How did you escape?'

'I kept on running until I got to the next village.'

'And then?'

'There were some friends. They took me in and alerted my brothers. Of course they went after our neighbours.' She paused and looked away. 'They burnt Tiga in the house, but Kerno got away. I don't know where he is now.'

'What would you do if you did?'

'I'd kill him,' said Edina simply. 'After we'd buried my mother, I didn't want to stay any more,' she added.

'Yet you loved the place.'

'Not any more. The land was contaminated. My brothers offered me a flat near them in the town. But I wanted to get out. Of course they tried to stop me by pointing out I didn't have any qualifications. One of my brothers is a journalist and I think that if I was going to do anything in England I'd want to write. Maybe become a specialist in writing about the Balkans, or even Seagate. But here I am still, eternally waiting. My brothers were right. I have no qualifications, no experience in journalism.' She paused. 'I wrote to the local paper – the *Seagate Observer* – and they put me on to this guy – a very nice guy called Carl Bennett – who is a journalist. We talked, but it was obvious my English wasn't good enough. I couldn't even speak the language that well, let alone write it. But now I'm better. At least I think I'm better.'

'You're very fluent. What do you think – what do you really think about Lorta's visit?'

'He's a puppet of the American government – and the UK. If they think they're going to have a second Tito then they are quite wrong. I don't think he's strong enough.'

'Do you know him?'

'A little.'

'What's he like?'

'My brothers knew him. Lorta's an intellectual, a theorist. He doesn't have grass-roots support.'

'So he won't do.'

'Nothing will do. Our country is at the mercy of several different factions.'

'Yet you love it.'

'No. I loved those foothills. Maybe I was retarded. I only wanted to live for the day – and watch the grass grow. What kind of person is that?'

'Someone who was happy.'

'A simpleton. Well, I'm not a simpleton any longer. I can assure you of that. I have my armour of cynicism. Look – if you've finished your tea, I must ask you to go. I'm very tired.'

Boyd sprang up.

'Do I make you nervous?' she asked.

'Yes,' said Boyd.

'Then I'm sorry. Thank you for hearing my story, but don't say you were privileged to hear it. Let's cut the bullshit.'

Boyd grinned at her. 'Your English *is* colloquial.'

'What does that mean?'

'It means you're speaking English as the English do.'

Boyd paused. 'Isn't Carl Bennett a member of this Ice Breakers club? The people who swim in the sea all the year round. Like Day?'

'Yes, he is. I told him he was mad. Maybe that didn't get him to like me too much.' She paused. 'Day. Why was he killed? Seagate seems to be getting like the Balkans. First of all a robbery and the death of a child. Then the murder of a local citizen.'

'It's hard to understand,' said Boyd. 'Maybe they are all coincidences.'

'So what do *you* think about Lorta's visit?' she asked. 'Can he be guaranteed full protection?'

'I'm sure the security services will look after Mr Lorta well enough,' said Boyd, and began to walk towards the door.

'Who are you, Mr James?' she asked softly.

Boyd froze. 'What do you mean by that?'

How had she found out?

For a few moments Boyd found himself unable to function. Then he turned round and saw that she was merely curious.

'No one is what they seem.'

'That's very enigmatic.' But he felt a sense of relief.

'We all wear a cloak of disguise. That's all I'm saying. By the way, have you met Jack King? He's another member of the Ice Breakers.'

'No.'

'He's a bastard.'

'Why?'

93

'He hates us. Really hates all asylum seekers.'

'What does this Jack King do?'

'He owns the amusement arcades – here in the town and on the pier. Our young people like to hang around them and he's always getting rid of them. They go inside for warmth in this freezing cold weather and they have little money. Not enough for Mr King anyway.'

Boyd was only half listening. What had she really meant when she had asked who he was?

'Go and see King. Tell him about Seekers. You should meet the local fascist,' said Edina. 'I'd like to know what you think of him.'

Chapter Ten

Boyd rang Hanley on his mobile as he stood outside the Grand, trying not to look at the mounting pile of flowers on the opposite side of Audley Square. If only more snow would fall, he thought, enough snow to cover those damnable flowers.

'I went to see Edina again.'

'What for?' Hanley sounded fractious.

'I wanted to get to know the central council a little better.'

'You met them this morning.'

'There was nothing for me to do.' Boyd knew he sounded defensive. 'I thought I'd use some initiative – just to get a little more background.'

'You should have asked me.'

'I'm sorry. Have I done something wrong?'

'No,' said Hanley quickly. 'How did you find Milstein?'

'Edina opened up a lot – told me the story of what happened to her – the terrible events that took place.'

'She tells that story to everyone. I'm not even sure if it's true. Please don't think I'm being critical of her. She needs help – therapy.' Hanley sounded oddly dismissive. 'But there are no funds for therapy.'

Boyd decided to remain silent and see how far Hanley was prepared to continue to deride Edina Milstein. Why was he doing it?

'It was a good idea to see her.' Suddenly Hanley seemed to want to be conciliatory.

'She suggested I meet Jack King. He hates all asylum seekers apparently. She calls him the Seagate fascist.'

'What the hell do you want to meet him for?' Now Hanley seemed anxious.

'I've got the asylum seekers' points of view. I might as well hear the opposition.'

'Aren't you exceeding your brief?'

'I only want to try and understand the situation – see it from all angles. Is that so wrong?'

Again Hanley seemed to want to back down. 'Of course. The rounded picture. I'm sorry. Harry Day's death has really got to me. He was such a good man.'

'Do the police know anything more about his murder?' Boyd deliberately used the word, but there seemed little reaction.

'Not that I've heard.'

'What does King think of Seekers?'

'Not a lot.'

'What doesn't he like about us?'

'He reckons we're just a bunch of do-gooders.'

'But Day was in the Ice Breakers. Surely he managed to explain –'

'They didn't get on,' said Hanley crisply.

'Yet they plunged into the icy seas together.'

'I don't think freezing cold immersion makes for togetherness – not in everything,' said Hanley drily.

'Be honest,' said Boyd, trying to be ameliorating. 'Do you feel I'm overstepping the mark?'

'Not at all.'

'I thought you seemed put out. I'd rather know –'

'I'm not in the least put out. Yes – go and see King. Try and sell him Seekers. Do your Christian duty.'

As Boyd switched his phone off, he wondered what kind of strain Hanley was under.

'Forty-forty,' said Arthur, raising his football to shoulder height. 'Forty-forty.'

'Why do you keep saying that?' Boyd walked up to him, his temper suddenly snapping. As if things weren't bad enough, he had to encounter this man again and again.

'Forty-forty,' he replied and walked briskly on.

Boyd watched him go, his temper cooling.

It was just after 6 p.m. when Boyd tried the first of Jack King's enterprises – the Family Fun Amusement Lounge on the seafront. He went up to the cash desk where a large, horrendously overweight man was thumbing through a copy of the *Mirror*.

'Is Mr King available?'

'Who wants him?'

'I'm Rick James, working for Seekers.'

The man gave a rich chuckle. 'I don't think he'll want to see you.'

'Why not?'

'Fucking do-gooder.'

Boyd smiled. 'I don't see myself like that.'

'How do you see yourself then?' he said curiously.

'As someone who's trying to understand the problems of the asylum seekers.'

'Wait a minute. I've heard about you. Aren't you a Christian? A fucking born-again Christian?'

'I *am* a Christian. But what's that to you?'

'Jack won't want to see you.'

'Well, just in case he does, where can I find him?'

'He'll be down at the pier tonight – in his office at the back of the arcade.'

'Thank you,' said Boyd. 'You've been very helpful.' He hurried out of the amusement lounge, all too conscious of his critic's mocking smile.

Seagate Pier hadn't had a coat of paint for a long time, and the rust had spread along the white balustrades right up to the scroll work at the top of a domed building on the decking. The woodwork in parts of the deck was so soft that they had been roped off, but surprisingly the gilded Victorian hulk was still open with free admission to the public.

Passing the Seekers office, Boyd walked down the full length of the pier, gazing at the faded grandeur that would surely soon fall into the sea. Down below, through holes in the deck, he could see the waves, dark and insistent, like a great sea cavern that boiled and lashed at the barnacle-hung pillars and stanchions.

'Mr James?'

He looked up to see a tall man with a weather-beaten face and a hatchet jaw. Boyd had never seen a hatchet jaw before. He thought such a phenomenon belonged to comics.

'I'm Major Jack King. I gather you're looking for me.'

'Yes.' Boyd was slightly thrown. He had expected to have a tough time finding him, but any hope that the conversation was going to be easier than he had thought was blown away immediately.

'There's really no point in you bothering to see me. I'm familiar with Seekers and, to be honest, I don't have any sympathy for your work.'

They both leant on the rusty railings and looked out at the night sea. A freezing wind was blowing and clouds were racing across the face of the moon.

'I've been told that, but I wanted to ask you why. Just for my own interest.'

Jack King sighed. 'You must appreciate how busy I am. But I can talk to you for a short time.'

'Thank you.'

'A very short time. Step this way.' He spoke with military authority and led Boyd into the welcome heat of an amusement arcade that had few punters – most of them asylum seekers who were contemplating the machines rather than playing them.

King opened the door of an extremely tidy office which

was dominated by a huge computer with a battery of attachments.

'Please sit down.'

'Thank you for talking to me.'

'As I said, I haven't much time.' Jack King looked down at his watch.

Boyd pressed on. 'I gather you are against the presence of the asylum seekers in this town – despite the fact that there are quite a few out there in your arcade.'

'I wouldn't describe half a dozen drifters as quite a few. They come in here for the warmth, but on a night like this I don't have the heart to throw them out.'

Boyd was surprised. He had expected a tirade. 'There don't seem to be many places they *can* go.'

'There's the library – which is now so full of them the locals can't read their newspapers. And there's me.'

'You own quite a few – enterprises in Seagate.'

'Yes. I wish I didn't. I can't get rid of them.'

'You mean they're up for sale?'

'Some of them. The ones I own. The others, like those on this pier, are leased from the local authority – and even harder to dispose of.'

'So you want to get out?'

'As fast as I can.'

'And you reckon the asylum seekers are the last straw?'

'You can say that again. I'm up to here with them, but I expect you've been told that. I'm known as the local fascist.'

Boyd was silent.

'For God's sake – we can't cope with our own unemployment and housing shortage, let alone take in a whole lot of waifs and strays. Seagate's becoming one big hostel for destitutes. It's an absolute slum.' King spoke briskly and oddly without malice.

'Wasn't it that way before?'

'We weren't exactly pulling in the punters,' said King impatiently, 'but the asylum seekers have really finished the town off. Who would want to come down to Seagate now? Even Dream World's closed.'

'Is that yours too?'

'It used to be, but I sold the place to City Security. They're an investment company which had originally hoped to redevelop the site – as well as the Grand. But who wants housing here now?'

'The asylum seekers I suppose.'

Jack King laughed emptily and then suddenly and surprisingly smiled at Boyd. 'Like a drink?'

'Thanks.'

'Scotch?'

'Yes, that would be nice.'

Jack King got up and went to a cupboard. 'Seagate needs regeneration. But would you invest in a clapped-out town like this? Of course, you might if there were some plans for light industry and employment, but those aren't even on the drawing board.'

'But there's always the hotel industry,' interrupted Boyd. 'Surely that's having something of a revival?'

'With six asylum seekers to a room – and the building partitioned off into the most inhumane living conditions. Come on – the situation is ridiculous. The dump has been dumped.'

'What about your own businesses?'

'Lousy. I was lucky to sell Dream World. We weren't even ticking over. I've got a bingo hall – that's still a sure-fire winner for the locals – and another arcade which is full of truanting kids and gives more warmth to your asylum seekers. And then there's this pier which is gradually falling into the sea. Soon the local authority are going to close it on the grounds that the structure's unsafe. I'm not a happy man, Mr James. I'm not a happy man at all. But I still don't think I'm a fascist.'

Neither did Boyd. In fact he rather liked Major King.

'What would you do with the asylum seekers if you had the power to settle their fate?' asked Boyd, sipping his whisky with an unaccustomed sense of well-being.

'Well, if they were sent back I can see some of them might face a sticky fate. I reckon we're stuck with them, but government policy should be to disperse them over the country. Everyone should be made to take the strain, not just derelict seaside towns with huge unemployment. That really *is* sweeping the problem under the carpet.'

'There's a lot in what you say. The town's obviously overwhelmed and now there's this murder –'

'Day.'

'Yes.' Boyd was silent and King cleared his throat.

'Day was convinced that some of the asylum seekers were being recruited by criminals and kept worrying at it. Hardly good for the health.' King laughed.

'Do you think that robbery had anything to do with the asylum seekers?'

'No way of telling.'

Boyd tried again. 'What did *you* think of Day?'

'What's this – a cross-examination?'

Boyd wasn't taken aback. Questions like this were an occupational hazard. 'I'm sorry. I'm just trying to get things in perspective. I'm very new to Seekers.'

'Are you salaried?'

'Barely.'

'Then what the hell are you doing there?'

'I've been in prison,' Boyd replied with what he hoped was a bleak honesty. 'I wanted to do something productive with my life.' He left out the born-again Christian bit, which he didn't think would go down too well with King.

'I see.'

But did he? wondered Boyd. 'I'm sorry about the questions. Shall I shut up?'

'Let me ask you one. What do you think of your boss? He's a rum sort of chap, isn't he?'

'I rather admire him. At least he believes in the cause.'

'I wish he wouldn't do it with hand-outs. It's the problem as a whole that needs addressing, not the odd individual.'

'There's always deserving cases – like Rila Kovac.'

'The woman whose son was killed by that getaway driver?'

'Yes.'

'She's had appallingly bad luck.' King got up and refilled their glasses.

'Do you think Day was right?' asked Boyd, wondering if King would accuse him of cross-examining him again.

'He could have been. All the asylum seekers are up for grabs. Take Rila Kovac for example.'

'What do you mean?' Boyd was immediately on the alert.

'She's desperate, isn't she? Now her boy's dead, she's lost any stability she might have had. And I'm sure whatever donation Seekers was able to give her was small. Even smaller than your salary. So she'll grab anything she can.' King paused. 'Hanley could find her useful.'

'In what way?'

'Did you know he was a police informer?'

King watched Boyd react with some amusement.

Chapter Eleven

Boyd was amazed. Why was King telling him, of all people? Unless he was out to undermine Seekers completely. Maybe this case was beginning to move after all. Boyd felt a rush of hopeful elation.

'That surprises you?'

'Of course.'

'I wonder,' said King drily. 'It occurs to me that an ex-con could be a useful recruit for Hanley. You could have your ear to the ground.'

'Are you seriously saying you think Seekers is just a vehicle for police surveillance?' Boyd hoped he sounded sufficiently outraged. 'If so, I don't like the idea of working for Hanley at all. I genuinely wanted to do something worthwhile for a change.'

'I didn't say I was giving you the facts. I'm talking about what I pick up on the grapevine. Seekers could well be what it says it is – a local charity handling an unpopular subject.'

'But you don't think so, do you?' Boyd felt he had to risk alienating King. The conversation had moved ahead so fast he had to capitalize on the momentum.

'For my money, Seekers is a front. It may have started as a well-meaning charity – I acquit Hilary Browning – but there's a lot of unrest amongst the asylum seekers at the moment and the security services could be using the agency to plug into the community, particularly in the light of Roma Lorta's impending visit.'

'What about the visit?' Boyd's mind was racing. Why

was Major King being so helpful? What did he really know?

'He's hardly popular.'

'Because he's a puppet of the British government?'

'And the US.'

'What are you expecting?'

'An assassination.'

'That's incredible!' Boyd hoped he sounded naively astonished.

'Don't be naive,' said King abrasively. 'The US and the UK are becoming manipulating partners in all too many international situations.'

'But Lorta's supposed to be visiting all the asylum-seeking refugees. Why are you so sure he'll be assassinated in Seagate?'

'I just have a hunch it's on the cards. And that brings me to another theory about Seekers.'

Who are you? wondered Boyd. Who the hell are you? You can't *just* be Major Jack King, the jovial owner of tatty amusement centres.

Then an incredible idea seeped into Boyd's mind. King apparently knew Hanley was a police informer. Suppose King was on the pay-roll as well? But if he was, surely Creighton would have told him. 'We've got a couple of plants in the town. They could be useful.' But Creighton had never mentioned King, so could King be working for someone else? The security services? MI6?

'You really think Seekers is just a front for the assassination of Lorta?' Boyd probed.

'It's a possibility.' Jack King laughed. 'But then you're here to sift through the theories, aren't you, Mr Boyd. I'm only giving you another one.'

A huge pit seemed to yawn in Boyd's stomach. How the hell had this happened? Wave after wave of panic surged through him as he gazed back at King in silence, wondering how he had blown this case away. But surely he'd done that from the start. After the boy.

'Stop worrying. I knew you were coming.' King seemed

to be trying to be reassuring. 'It was just a question of how long you'd take to get to me.'

'Who are you?' Boyd tried to sound assertive, but he knew he was failing.

'Major Jack King.'

'But who else?'

'No one else. I've been in Seagate for ten years – and I really do try to amuse.'

'Who set you up?'

'Creighton. I've worked for him before. In London. Now I cover the south-east.'

'You're a police officer?'

'No way.'

'An insider?'

'Wrong again. I'm like Hanley. I inform. After all, I know a lot of people.'

'So you and Hanley work together.'

'You must be joking. Hanley's a straw in the wind,' said King impatiently. 'I'm a professional and I get a professional fee.'

'So Hanley doesn't know anything about you – about that side of you?'

'And I want to keep it that way.' King paused. 'And then there were three. You, me and Hanley, but we play very different roles. You're the activist. I'm the listener. Hanley gathers bird seed.'

Boyd was wondering if King knew about the purpose of the raid. How much *did* he know? Were all three of them kept in a certain well-defined ignorance? In their separate compartments?

'Creighton should have told me. Put me right in the picture from the start.'

'Sure as hell he shouldn't. It's a golden rule that the less we know about each other the better. You know that.'

'So why reveal yourself now?'

'It suited me. Hanley has an ear to the asylum seekers,' said King impatiently. 'I've got the local knowledge. And you're action man.' He paused and then said, 'It was a pity about Stefan.'

Boyd looked away, disappointed that he knew. More than disappointed. He felt exposed and contemptible, as he should.

King was silent, and Boyd was grateful.

'I feel terrible about the boy.'

'It was an accident.'

'That doesn't make it any better.'

'No,' said King with a sudden certainty. 'It wouldn't.'

'Were you going to approach me if I hadn't come to you?'

Jack King shrugged. 'I wanted to see what you would do. I needed to know how good you were.'

'And?'

'You seem OK to me.' He sounded unimpressed.

'Thanks.'

'What's the betting you'll be on the phone to Creighton directly you leave me?' Jack King got up and shook his hand. 'I'm glad we talked. Can I have your mobile number?'

Boyd hesitated. 'Why?'

'Because I'm afraid.'

'What of?'

'One Ice Breaker down, two to go.'

'There's just the three of you?' asked Boyd.

'The others aren't really tough enough. They're not consistent.'

'Do you need protection?'

'I'd like to see what's available.' For the first time King betrayed fear.

Boyd was startled. 'Who's after you?'

'I wish I knew.'

'Do you know who killed Day?'

'Not the person who killed him.'

'What do you mean?' Boyd was getting anxious.

'As the Queen told her butler – there are dark forces in England.'

'Can't you be more specific?'

'If our dear Queen can't elaborate, how could I?' He grinned evasively at Boyd. 'But I'd like some protection. Next time you report back.'

'I'll do it right away,' said Boyd.

Boyd called Creighton on his mobile from the other end of the promenade where the cliffs overhung a large car park. He wasn't immediately available so Boyd walked over to the sea. It was high tide and the waves were grinding over the pebbles, the surging strangely comforting.

Eventually Creighton called him back. 'Where are you?'

'On a particularly bleak beach.'

'Sounds fun.'

'I'm not having any fun.'

'Something gone wrong?'

'Jack King went wrong. I thought he was a fascist. Now I understand he's another informer. Wasn't Hanley enough?'

'That's correct.'

'You hadn't felt like telling me?'

'Not until you'd dug yourself in. You're our man on the spot who stirs the pot.'

'Thank you. You don't think you're rather packing Seagate with operatives?' Boyd was bitter.

'As far as I'm aware there's no one else – but, as you can imagine, Faraday must have other snouts. Hanley and King were infiltrated a long time ago – and not just by me.'

'Do either of them know who killed Day?' asked Boyd.

'If they did, King would have told you – and Hanley would have told Faraday.'

'What a complicated web you weave,' began Boyd.

'When we practise to deceive,' finished Creighton.

Boyd stared morosely at the sea, wondering why he'd

involved himself in all this. But of course the answer was obvious.

'I think something's imminent,' said Creighton.

'Lorta's assassination. But the question is, who's going to do it? The asylum seekers themselves, or a hired man?'

'You seem to have worked out the options,' said Creighton.

'King wants protection.'

'Did he say why?'

'There are only three full-time members of Ice Breakers. One down, with possibly two to go. I think King is afraid. You'll need to help him out.'

'I'll do what I can.' Creighton was annoyed.

Boyd looked down the beach and saw that it was beginning to snow again. The flakes were large and white in the darkness, falling slowly, relentlessly. He felt a sudden despair for he knew he would never get a grip on this situation until he got a grip on Rick James. The mantle was too slippery, too alien. In the past he had been able to draw on a false identity fairly easily. But now his new mantle had evaded him for the first time.

'Snowing again,' said Major King as his office door was opened.

'I wanted to speak to you,' said his visitor.

'Fire away.'

'Not in here.'

'For God's sake – haven't you noticed the state of the weather out there?'

'Something's happened. Something bad. We need to talk.'

'I don't want to catch my death,' said King, getting to his feet. 'So be quick about it.'

The snow was falling thickly as Boyd walked back towards

the promenade. Dimly, through the driving snowflakes he could just see someone stumbling over the pebbles, several times almost falling. Then the figure was blotted out as the snow fell faster and the flakes became a white screen.

Boyd screwed up his eyes and suddenly realized the stumbling figure was Major Jack King.

'I thought I might find you here. I need your help.' King's voice was slightly muffled and he was wheezing badly.

'Creighton says he's going to lay on some protection.' King staggered again and then went down on his knees, clutching at his chest. 'I'm afraid he's too late.'

'For Christ's sake –' Boyd gazed down at King. He was wearing a light grey overcoat that was heavily stained.

King was gasping for breath now, fumbling at the buttons of his coat.

'What is it?' Boyd crunched quickly over the snow-covered pebbles towards him.

'I've had a visitor.'

One of the lamps on the promenade came on and in its pale glow Boyd saw that King had undone his coat buttons and was trying to pull something out of his chest.

'For Christ's sake!' Boyd saw the knife too late. The knife that was buried up to the hilt in his chest. 'Leave the fucking thing alone.'

King began to cough and within a few moments blood was pouring from his mouth. Again he tugged at the knife and the wheeze became a lethal rasping.

'Don't touch the thing!' Boyd repeated, grabbing at King's bloodied hand.

'Have – to – get – it – out –'

'No!' Boyd dragged out his mobile and began to punch in the number for the emergency services. He got an immediate response, gave the location and rammed the mobile back in his pocket. Boyd turned back to King to find he was still struggling with the knife. 'No!' Boyd yelled again. 'Leave it where it is. For God's sake, leave it.'

But King had finally pulled it out, leaving a ragged hole in his chest from which dark blood poured.

Boyd dragged a handkerchief out of his pocket and tried to pad the ragged hole and stop the steady stream of blood.

But the blood simply pumped straight through.

Boyd pulled off his coat and sweater, pressing the sweater over the hole although he knew there was very little he could do. The wound in King's chest was enormous. Surely no one could survive that?

Taking him in his arms Boyd lowered King on to the pebbles until he was lying on his back.

'You're going to be all right,' said Boyd. 'Keep hanging in there.' The words echoed in his head with stunning banality. He was sweating, despite the cold, still shocked by the sudden horror of it all. 'Hold on.' Boyd was pressing down on the bloodied sweater even harder, and although it had little effect he didn't know what else to do. 'The ambulance is on its way.'

'Don't need one,' said King. There was a rattling in his throat and his eyes opened wide in the pale light. 'I needed protection,' he said. 'I should have sought you out.'

'What about Faraday?'

'He doesn't run me.' King's breathing was becoming a rasp. 'Is it bad?' he asked.

'Yes,' said Boyd.

'The trouble with me –' King was whispering now – 'is that I always leave things too late.'

'Who did this?'

'They were quite clever.' King seemed surprised. 'Much more resourceful than I supposed.' He began to cough up blood.

'The ambulance is coming,' said Boyd.

'They'll be too late,' replied King. His eyes glazed and the coughing became a long drawn-out rasp that faltered and then died away.

I've lost him, thought Boyd. He tried mouth-to-mouth resuscitation but failed. He sat back on his haunches, gasping for breath, listening to the low growling of the tiny waves on the pebbles. Looking down at King's torn chest Boyd hesitated, wondering if he dared to try and restart his heart. To hell with his injury, he thought. I've got to get him back. But Boyd crouched there, still doing nothing, knowing there was nothing he could do.

Then he heard the sirens and for a moment relief flooded him. King was no longer his responsibility.

Chapter Twelve

'I'm DI Faraday,' gasped the police officer who was over-weight and out of breath.

There were a large number of police officers on the pebbles now, while a couple of paramedics lifted King's body on to a stretcher.

'You know who I am,' said Boyd.

'I'll need to check your ID.'

Boyd passed him his mobile and gave Faraday a number. Eventually he got through to Creighton, received confirmation and gave the phone back to Boyd.

'What happened?' asked Faraday.

'I don't know. I came down here to think after talking to King. He was very open with me, surprisingly open. It turns out that he's an informer too. Been doing it a long time apparently. No one told me.' Boyd paused. 'Which brings me to Hanley.'

'We know about Hanley. But no one told me about King. Does Creighton know?'

'Yes.'

'Typical.'

'King was certainly more in touch with the criminal underworld than Hanley, but Hanley's job brings him closer to the asylum seekers.'

'Looks like we've lost an important player,' said Faraday calmly. 'You'd better tell me what happened.'

'I'd been talking to King in his office on the pier. He revealed that he was an informer and said he knew I was

112

working undercover. I left him in the office and went to this car park to speak to Creighton on my mobile.'

'Checking.'

'Complaining.'

'And then?'

'King came down to the beach. He was staggering towards me, trying to pull that fucking great knife out of his chest. I told him not to touch it but the damage was done. He died on me.'

'Did he say if he recognized his attacker?'

'No.'

'Any detail at all?'

'Nothing.'

'You're not holding out on me?'

'Why should I?'

'Because you're undercover. I've had problems with your lot before.'

'I can assure you I've told you everything. The bank raid was of course a set-up – an attempt to indicate that I was a criminal and up for hire. It didn't work – and you know the repercussions.'

'Officially I'm in the middle of an investigation on that raid.'

'But you knew –'

'From the start. Has anyone contacted you?'

'Not a soul.'

'God, what a mess,' said Faraday. 'Maybe the assassin's already in place.'

'That's what I'm worried about,' admitted Boyd.

'And despite all this surveillance, I've got two murders on my hands and very few leads. How the hell am I meant to protect Lorta?'

'I'm sorry,' said Boyd again. 'But it's not down to me. Maybe you should complain to someone – like Creighton. He's in charge of the shadow play.'

'OK. I'm not saying that it's your fault.' Suddenly Faraday seemed flustered. 'But I'd like to be kept in the picture.'

'That goes for me too.' Boyd paused. 'Maybe you can give me some information now.'

'I'll try.'

'What links Day and King?'

'Membership of the Ice Breakers – a winter sea swimming club.'

'Is that relevant?'

'To keep them in touch perhaps.'

'But what's the link between the murders? Unless there's someone out there who doesn't like people indulging in a spot of winter swimming? A penguin maybe.'

'Any more inappropriate jokes?' Faraday was disapproving.

'Suppose they both knew more than they should about the assassination attempt?'

'Yes,' said Faraday, slowly and patiently. 'But what?'

King's body had long since been removed, and Boyd and Faraday were alone on the bleak snow-swept beach in the dark.

'How are you coping?' asked Faraday unexpectedly.

'Coping?'

'You killed the child. Remember?'

For a moment Boyd thought he was going to hit him. Then with great difficulty he controlled himself. 'You do your job, I do mine.'

Faraday looked across at the caravan which had just been set up on the promenade marked POLICE INCIDENT ROOM. 'We're capable of a lot more than you think. Us locals.'

'Salt of the earth,' muttered Boyd.

'I think we should go our separate ways now,' said Faraday. 'But we do need to keep in touch. This situation is running out of control. So go undercover and stop surfacing.'

'I don't need any advice from you. I know exactly what I have to do.' If only that was true, Boyd thought involuntarily.

*   *   *

114

He slept badly that night, dreaming of Stefan again, seeing him fall in the snow under the spinning wheels of the getaway van. Tossing and turning, unable to sleep, he felt increasingly trapped by the enormity of what he had done. Eventually he made up his mind to go and see Rila the next morning and try to help her personally rather than through Seekers. But then he realized he couldn't possibly do anything of the kind.

Walking through the snow-bound streets, Boyd came to a decision. Now King was dead, he had to confront Hanley and he was damned if he'd get permission from Creighton first. King had come clean, so why shouldn't he force Hanley to do the same?

As he made his way towards the Seekers office at the head of the pier he saw in his mind's eye a dense woodland through which he was slowly and painfully hacking a path. Then, to his irritation, he noticed an old friend standing on the promenade, near the police incident caravan and the roped-off section of the beach where King had died.

'Forty-forty,' said Arthur, his football raised in a strong right hand. 'Forty-forty.'

'You look shagged out,' said Hanley.

'That's how I feel.'

'You heard about King?'

'On the radio,' said Boyd.

'They're talking about a serial killer.' Hanley sounded incredulous.

'They?'

'The media.' He passed across a copy of the *Guardian*.

The small, black headline read: SERIAL KILLER AT SEAGATE.

During the last forty-eight hours Seagate, a small town by the sea in south-east England, has seen two killings. The first body to be found, washed up on the pebble beach, was fifty-two-year-old Harry Day, a local bank manager and president of the charity known as Seekers.

Based in Seagate, the charity provides help for the large numbers of asylum seekers living in the town.

Early last night, Major Jack King, a local businessman, was stabbed and found dying on the beach by one of the staff of Seekers.

DI Faraday of Seagate CID commented, 'These are early days in our investigation and to link the two men's deaths is premature, although they were both members of the Ice Breakers, a winter swimming club.'

Seagate has one of the densest populations of asylum seekers in the country and is currently awaiting a visit from Roma Lorta, the soon to return exiled President of Lubic, the smallest of the Balkan states created from the former Yugoslavia.

Seagate is also an area of high unemployment.

'Implications?' said Boyd as he put down the paper.

Hanley shrugged.

'The implications are that the Lorta visit and the asylum seekers could be connected with the killings.'

Hanley didn't reply and after a long silence Boyd continued.

'Who could have murdered Day and King? Was it the same person, and if so, why?'

'They might both have known something,' Hanley suggested.

'What about?'

'Lorta?'

'Are you saying Day and King knew something about an assassination plot?'

'Possibly. I've already had Faraday here. He's taken away a lot of files.'

'What about?'

'The cases we've assisted with over the last year.'

'I'm sure they'll be a lot of help,' said Boyd drily.

Hanley shrugged. 'Faraday seemed to think a plot to kill

Lorta was on the cards and that a group of asylum seekers might be involved.'

'I suppose Day could have got wind of something, but King spent his time keeping the asylum seekers at a distance, and despite the Ice Breaker connection I can't really see them working together on anything.'

'You wouldn't think so, would you?' said Hanley. 'But things are running out of control. First of all that bank raid and the tragedy of the child, then the fears about Lorta's visit and now these murders.'

Taking advantage of Hanley's apparent agitation, Boyd pressed on. 'How well did you know Day? And King?'

'I knew Harry Day pretty well. He'd been my bank manager ever since I came to Seagate and, of course, the Seekers account was with him. He was a decent man with strong family ties. Sadly he was an early widower. His wife died of cancer a few years ago.'

'What was his attitude to the asylum seekers?'

'He was a liberal. Harry was concerned about the high numbers of asylum seekers we have in Seagate, but he was really worried about the bad conditions they're living in – like the Grand, for instance. He was always lobbying the local authority, and the Ministry come to that. But he never really got anywhere and I knew he was beginning to feel as defeated as I did. Some of the asylum seekers thought he was ineffective, but I can't imagine why anyone should want to murder him. If it wasn't for King, I'd still be prepared to stick to the possibility of an accident.' Hanley paused. 'Tell me what happened.'

'He came out of nowhere. There wasn't anything I could do for him. I was on the beach, watching the sea, having a think.'

'In the dark?'

'Why not?'

'In freezing conditions?'

'So?' Boyd suddenly realized he was being counter-interrogated and smiled inwardly, appreciating the irony of the situation.

'So it was just coincidence that King died on you?'

'No,' replied Boyd. 'I'd been talking to him.'

'Did Jack King tell you anything – anything of importance?' Hanley probed.

Boyd side-stepped the question. 'I rather liked him. I didn't think King was a fascist at all.'

'What was he then?'

Boyd suddenly decided to take the risk. 'I gather he was a police informer.'

'How do you know that?' Hanley sounded only vaguely interested.

'He told me.'

'Why ever should he do that?'

'He also told me something I could hardly believe.'

'What was that?'

'He told me you were an informer too.'

Chapter Thirteen

'King told you I was an informer?' Hanley seemed relieved but bemused. 'I wonder how many other people he told. And how did he know in the first place?'

'Because he was an informer too, but on a wider scale I think.'

'Christ!' Hanley seemed genuinely shocked. 'Who was he reporting to? Faraday?'

'No. I think he was being employed by one of the security services.'

'Why?'

'Because of Lorta. Because it's on the cards he'll be the victim of an assassination attempt.'

'But that's only a recent possibility. King's been here a long time.'

'So have the asylum seekers. And they're like stones on a beach. They seem to be just part of the seascape, but we don't know what's under them.'

'You can say that again.'

'He claimed you kept the police informed about the asylum-seeker community.'

'Yes,' Hanley admitted. 'I've given information to the police for quite some while now.' He still sounded relieved.

'Ever since you joined Seekers?' asked Boyd.

'Yes.'

'What were you doing before you started working at Seekers and turned informer?' Boyd knew he must sound suspiciously social – as if he had just met Hanley at a function and was making small talk.

'I never *turned* informer. I had access to certain lines of information the police were interested in.'

'And still are?'

'Of course.' Hanley paused. 'But everyone's clammed up lately. I assure you I don't make much money out of disseminating information. But to answer your question, I was a social worker and probation officer before I took up this job.'

'In Seagate?'

'In Hastings – there are similarities.' Hanley paused. 'The current situation's extremely volatile and I failed to deliver. Presumably King did too, or they wouldn't have brought you in, Mr James – although I'm sure that's not your real name.'

Despite the fact that Boyd had continually expected an approach from Hanley, he hadn't even considered the possibility of Hanley approaching him as an upholder of law and order.

'You certainly took your time in approaching me.' Boyd looked at him curiously. 'I wondered what you were playing at.'

'Just being careful. You may have noticed that any mistakes around here tend to be fatal.'

Boyd got up and wandered over to the window, gazing out at the snow-clad promenade and pier. There was no sign of any let-up in the freeze.

'I need protection.' Hanley suddenly sounded desperate. 'First Day and now King. What's the betting I'm next on the list?'

'I can't offer you protection until I talk to my boss.' Boyd came and sat down again.

'Do that right away.'

'Is there something you haven't told me?'

'No. But someone might think I know more than I do.'

Boyd went back to the window and dialled Creighton's

number on his mobile. This time he got through first time.

'I'm with Hanley.'

'I gather you've been in the thick of it.'

'You could say that. Hanley knows – and in the light of recent events admits to feeling completely exposed. He's asking for protection.'

'I'll authorize that with Faraday. Two murders in two days. You need to be careful.' Creighton sounded anxious. 'I think this Lorta visit should be cancelled.'

'Can that be done?'

'I don't know. I'm going to try. As to Hanley, that's an easier task. Keep an eye on him until Faraday gets in touch.'

Boyd turned back to Hanley. 'Faraday will be in touch. Meanwhile I'm not to let you out of my sight.'

'So I've got protection?'

'You will have. But for the moment you've got me.' Boyd sat down again.

'That robbery was a set-up, wasn't it?' asked Hanley.

'Yes.'

'To draw exactly who out of the woodwork?'

'Someone who might want to employ me as an assassin. The point is,' Boyd added, 'two men have already been murdered – maybe for what they knew – so an assassin could already be in place.' Boyd felt a surge of disappointment and a feeling of failure. He had been put into Seagate to take up a criminal offer, maybe the role of assassin. But now someone else had claimed the job. 'Are you sure you don't know something yourself that could be dangerous?'

'Yes.' Hanley was adamant.

'If you're holding anything back it could be fatal, not only for Lorta but for you as well. I do think you've got to be more realistic. What have you *really* been telling the police?'

'I told you – only the activities of some of the asylum seekers,' said Hanley vaguely, and Boyd felt a surge of

121

anger. For God's sake, what was the matter with Hanley? Two men were dead and he knew he could be the next on the list. But he was *still* keeping the cards close to his chest.

'And there wasn't anything significant – nothing I should know about?'

'No. I told them about some new asylum seekers arriving. I think they came from Macedonia. One of them has a history of violent crime.'

'Who is he?'

'Milo Rodensky. He's been here a few days now.'

'Living where?'

'At the Grand.'

'Anything more?'

'There is something I told Faraday which we haven't touched on.'

At last, thought Boyd. 'Well?'

'Carl Bennett.'

'Who's he?'

'A reporter on the local rag – the *Seagate Observer*.'

'I've glanced at it. But I don't remember seeing the name Bennett.'

'It's not prominently displayed in the paper. Not any more,' said Hanley.

'Any reason?'

'Chambers – the owner of the *Observer* – he doesn't like campaigning journalists, particularly those who campaign for asylum seekers.'

'And is this what Bennett does?'

'Yes. Or at least he used to. Of course the material went right against local opinion and stirred up a lot of trouble.'

'You mean Bennett supported the rights of the community here?'

'Every week. He really knocked it home – about the length of time they have to wait, the conditions in which they live and a lot more about their identities and roots. Just what everyone in Seagate wants to hear.'

'Especially when there's a huge unemployment problem,' added Boyd.

'He wrote about that too. The necessity for a bypass for the town and a motorway link to London so that there would be a chance for expanding light industry here. But he still wrote more about the asylum seekers than he did about local affairs.'

'Why did Chambers go along with that?'

'Initially he thought the *Observer* might sell more copies because of the controversy.'

'Not just to become more radical, more cause-orientated?'

'That's not Chambers's line.'

'So what happened?'

'Bennett's column was dropped.'

'And has he gone?'

'No – he's still on the paper.'

'I'm surprised he agreed to stay,' said Boyd.

'I reckon he's hanging on for the Lorta visit. Chambers can't stop him reporting that.'

'Or selling copy to the nationals?'

'That too.'

'What's Bennett like? An idealist?'

'No – he's one hundred per cent realistic. He told me we're on the edge of anarchy in Seagate.'

'With the Lorta visit?'

'Not just that. The conditions are so bad, the prejudice of the local people, the feeling of being dumped and dumped on. Surely a tide of violence has begun.'

'Maybe that could have been the reason behind Bennett's campaigning journalism,' said Boyd thoughtfully. 'Has it occurred to you that Bennett could have been manipulating the local community to bump up his lineage?'

'Bennett's not like that,' said Hanley furiously. 'He understands the asylum seekers' problems, and in my job here at Seekers I really appreciated that.'

'So that was what you told Faraday then. Hardly a revelation.'

'About as useful as your alias,' Hanley agreed maliciously.

'What's that supposed to mean?' asked Boyd angrily.

'It means that, after a while, after too short a while, you began to take the initiative rather too much for an ex-con. And why the hell did they give you that born-again cover? Wasn't that something of a liability?'

'It was a mistake,' snapped Boyd. 'We all make them. Even my boss.' He paused. 'Are you saying my cover's blown?'

'Not with the council.' Hanley sounded less hostile now. 'They all like and accept you. At least Edina Milstein does.'

'What more can I get out of her?'

'Quite a lot more. She likes to be talked to. She's very thick with Bennett – one of his primary sources.'

'I'll go and see her again. But I need another pretext.'

'Go and talk about the arrangements for Lorta's visit and the community's own security arrangements.'

'Isn't that out of order?'

'God, no. Seekers has always encouraged the community to police itself.'

There was a knock on the door and Hanley jumped to his feet.

'Maybe your protection's arrived.' Boyd walked over to the door, paused and opened it very quickly.

A young man in a dark suit and overcoat stood on the threshold.

'I'm DI Jon Martin from Seagate CID.' He showed Boyd his ID and came through to shake hands with Hanley. 'Don't worry, sir. I'll be within sight of you twenty-four hours a day – or at least me or my relief will.'

'I'm glad to hear it,' said Hanley, turning to Boyd. 'If you're going to see Edina Milstein again, I suggest you go now.' He sounded much more decisive.

'Want to come?'

'No. I'm not in a position to play social calls at present. She might find the presence of my new minder a little inhibiting. We need to know what security the community has in mind.'

'Maybe they expect policing to be the police's job.'

'That's for you to find out,' snapped Hanley.

'Mr James. Back so soon?'

'I've come on another matter – on behalf of Mr Hanley.'

'What do you want?' Edina's voice was sharp. 'I'm very busy.'

'I want to talk about Lorta's visit.'

'From whose point of view?'

'The council's.'

'We've already spoken to the police about that.'

'Seekers would be grateful for some idea of what's going on. I think we've earned that right by now.' Boyd met her hostility head on, which seemed to work for she immediately became more co-operative.

'I'm sorry. Of course you must know what's going on. The charity has made so many efforts on our behalf.' Somehow she implied that Seekers had completely failed to deliver. 'You'd better come in.'

The room was rather untidier than before with a number of Slavic books scattered over the sofa.

'I've been trying to work out how many different languages we muster between us,' she said.

'Are you using interpreters?'

'We can't afford that. What do you expect? Simultaneous translation?'

'I didn't think you'd run to that.' Boyd hurried on clumsily. 'I gather you're using the Grand. That could be difficult to make secure. Isn't there a larger, more containable venue in the town?'

'I don't think he'd be very welcome in the town hall.'

'Have you tried anywhere else?'

125

'Yes, and been refused – and, yes, it's been made very clear we wouldn't be welcome.'

'I'm sorry to hear that.'

'And I'm horrified to hear what's been going on. Day – and now King. Do *you* think there's a serial killer in Seagate, Mr James?'

'I don't know.'

'Don't you have an opinion?'

'Mr Hanley's concerned that some criminal element's getting in on the act and clearing away the opposition.'

'What act?'

'Your act.'

'Whatever do you mean?'

'Someone might be intending to carry out an assassination. Or making an arrangement with someone to become an assassin. Lorta's an ambiguous figure, as you told me yourself, and not to everyone's taste.'

'Whatever I may have said, I'm quite sure there won't be any violence on our part. Not here in Seagate. Not after what we've all been through,' she added.

'Can you give me an idea of the overall plan?' Boyd sat down in one of the armchairs, but Edina remained standing.

'Lorta will arrive at about two in the afternoon tomorrow and talk to the members of our community in the ballroom here at the Grand.'

'Do you mind if we go and take another look?'

'I'm not sure why – or what you need to know. He'll come with his own bodyguards,' she said dismissively.

Boyd simulated a sigh of relief. Then he had an idea. 'I suppose it wouldn't be possible for Seekers to attend the meeting?'

'I don't understand . . .' She seemed immediately agitated and Boyd wondered why.

'Would you object to Mr Hanley, or me, being present – and maybe saying a word about the objectives of the charity?'

'I see. You want to get something out of this too.' She gave Boyd a bitter smile.

'To let Lorta know what we're here for and what we've been doing.'

'And what we're up against here – forced out of our homeland and treated like shit in this so-called liberal country.'

'Something like that,' said Boyd.

'But at least that fascist bastard King got a knife in his gut at last,' she said viciously.

'Chest, actually. But –'

'Of course, you were there. How very unpleasant. Did he die on you?'

'Pretty much so.'

'How very unpleasant,' she repeated.

'I got the paramedics, but they couldn't save him.'

'Well, don't expect me to grieve. I'm not such a hypocrite.'

'I went to talk to him as you suggested. I think you may have read him wrong,' said Boyd. There was a long silence. Then he asked, 'And what about my request?'

'For you to sell your charity –'

'You've got the wrong word.' Boyd wanted to put her down, however childishly.

'I'm joking. You want to represent your charity.'

'If possible.'

'Well, I'm sure that will be OK by us. I'll have to put your request to the council of course.' She looked at him sharply. 'You're holding something back, Mr James.'

'The police may cancel Lorta's visit,' he replied hurriedly.

Edina was immediately furious. 'Who told you that?'

'Mr Hanley.'

'Oh, don't listen to him – he's a revolting little man.'

'Why do you say that?' At once Boyd was curious.

'He's full of self-importance. Never really knows anything, but pretends he does. I can't stand the type.' She paused. 'We can look at the ballroom now if you like. Then you can see where you might position yourself – if the council agree, of course.'

Boyd knew that any agreement would be down to her.

More of the plaster from the ceiling had fallen on to what had once been a deep pile red carpet. Now whole sections of the carpet had disintegrated, exposing a wooden floor.

'That's better,' said Boyd.

'What is?' asked Edina impatiently.

'The wooden floor. You could strip off that carpet completely.'

'We've already tried, but the carpet's so damp it's stuck to the floor. Better to cover the bare patches with rugs.' She looked at him and gave a rather forced smile. 'I didn't realize you were so fascinated by interior design.'

'Design's the only interesting thing about Seagate. Everything's rotting, but inside and out you can still see the style.'

'Yes,' she agreed grudgingly. 'I like the Grand. It reminds me of a hotel I knew in Sarajevo, also slowly decaying. But the Grand is slipping away much faster and I don't think renovation's possible. Not any more. I feel the same way about myself.' Edina smiled ruefully and Boyd grinned, making eye contact with her for the first time.

'Do you expect to be given British citizenship?' asked Boyd abruptly.

'If I go home my life will be in danger. Or is that what they all say?'

Boyd didn't want to give her a direct answer. 'Could you settle here?'

'Maybe. But at the moment I'm more afraid than I was in the Balkans.'

'Are you talking about the murders?' he asked gently.

'More than the murders. It's as if everyone in Seagate's waiting. Waiting passively like all British people do. Waiting for all of us to be blown away.'

'What are you saying?'

'There's so much resentment here.'

'There's bound to be some.'

'I'm not talking about some. I'm talking about everybody. We're seen as scum. Foreign scum at that. No one realizes a lot of us are professional people who had good jobs at home.'

'Nonsense.'

'But it's true.'

'If you're talking about scum – you're talking about the residents of Seagate. This is the end of the line. This is where no-hopers come to die.'

'Yes, but they're bitter no-hopers. We're taking up their space.'

Boyd decided to try and use her sudden openness. 'You *are* concerned about Lorta's safety, aren't you?'

'Very.'

'What do you think's going to happen?'

Edina pulled out of her pocket a couple of letters and gave them to Boyd. They were addressed to the council and were made up from letters cut from a newspaper. Boyd fleetingly wondered if it was the *Seagate Observer*.

The wording was crude.

Get back to where you came from you foreign cunt.

Fuck off, dirty dago.

'Dago?' Boyd was amused. 'I think they've got the wrong country.'

Edina laughed. 'You're right. They're the scum. Ignorant scum. But also dangerous.'

'Do you know this journalist guy? What's his name? Bennett?'

'Carl Bennett. He's one of the few good men in this town. He supported our cause, until he was smothered by that foul bastard Chambers.'

'Did he think Bennett was inflammatory?'

'Chambers thought Bennett lost him readers. And of course he did.'

129

Now that Edina was so fired up, Boyd decided to return to the killings.

'Day and King. There doesn't seem to be much of a link.'

'King was a fascist bastard.'

'So you say. But you can't cast Day in the same mould.'

'I'm not so sure. I could feel his hostility.'

'But he was president of Seekers.' Boyd was surprised. This was the first time he'd heard Day criticized.

'I've never seen Seekers as effective. Bennett did a better job.'

'I'm sorry to hear that,' said Boyd. 'Maybe I can work harder and impress you.'

Edina shrugged. 'I hate the way you want to help me.'

'Why?' asked Boyd.

'In other circumstances we would have been more equal.'

Boyd smiled at her and fleetingly she smiled back.

'Stefan. That was a dreadful episode.' She looked harassed now and Boyd inwardly cringed.

'I must go and see his mother again.' He felt hugely vulnerable, certain that the fatal result of his criminal carelessness would reverberate for ever.

'I should keep away from her.'

'Why?'

'She needs her dignity.'

'Do I just seem patronizing?'

'Send your money. Don't take it in person.'

'That's what she would like?'

But Edina didn't reply. Instead, she said, 'If I could ever get hold of the bastard who killed Stefan –'

'It was an accident,' said Boyd. 'They set out to rob a bank – not to kill a child.' Then he wished he hadn't said anything.

Edina gave him a searching look. 'How do you know that?'

'It's obvious.'

'There was something wrong,' she said.

Boyd froze. 'What do you mean?'

'About that robbery.'

'What do you think was wrong?' he asked, trying to stay calm.

'Maybe you were right when you said something had to be financed.'

'Something?'

'An assassination.'

'That's why I was asking all those questions about security,' said Boyd

'I'm sure we can look after Lorta.' She was impatient again. 'We'll do that. There's no need to worry. Where would you like your Seekers help desk?'

'I didn't say it was going to be a help desk. We'd just like to be a presence. To make sure your leader realizes Seagate isn't all hostile and that efforts *are* being made, however ineffective. We mean to recruit more staff.'

'There's something about your boss that I just don't like,' she began again.

But Boyd knew it was time to go. 'I'd better get back to the office. Thanks very much for showing me round. If you'll put the idea of having a Seekers presence here tomorrow afternoon to the council I'd be very grateful. Perhaps you could give me or Mr Hanley a ring tomorrow?'

'Of course. But I'm sure my colleagues aren't going to object.'

'Thank you. We'd be very pleased to –'

'Fly the flag.'

'Something like that,' said Boyd uncomfortably.

Chapter Fourteen

The snow was melting, becoming a grey slush. But Boyd could still see hard lumps of ice in places where the sun hadn't penetrated. When he arrived at the pier, he went straight to the office and reported to Hanley, who was sitting behind his desk examining a pile of papers. He shoved one of them over to Boyd.

'I'm designing a new brochure – and a mission statement. I can have it run off for Lorta's visit.'

Boyd cast a distracted eye over the copy which began WE SEEK TO HELP. He didn't want to read any more.

'I've seen Edina. She made it clear that visiting Rila again would be seen as patronizing.'

'And what about Edina? Did she have anything to say about the security arrangements for Lorta?'

'Not a lot. She just emphasized that the council could handle it. But I think she'll be able to get us into the meeting. She agreed to call tomorrow and let us know.'

'Maybe you should go.'

'I think we should both be there. The point is, whatever they say, I think you should talk to Faraday about security.'

'I've already spoken to Faraday. Lorta's visit is to go ahead and there'll be more than adequate security. He's liaising with Special Branch.'

'OK,' said Boyd. 'Bennett's next on my list. I'll try to make an appointment to see him. Have you any idea what his real motives in supporting the asylum seekers might be?'

Hanley gave him a sour smile. 'As I've already told you, there's no problem with Bennett. Maybe he's ambitious, but as far as the asylum seekers in Seagate are concerned he really did try to get his readers to understand them. Until Chambers put his spoke in.'

'What kind of man is Chambers?'

'A bullshitter – a liberal. He owns property in the town.'

'Inhabited by asylum seekers?'

'Chambers is a partner in the investment company that owns the Grand. When the asylum seekers are out of the building his company intends to tear the place down.'

'And replace it with what?'

'I've no idea.'

'It's a pity that we couldn't have revealed our positions earlier and pooled information,' said Boyd impatiently. 'Maybe these killings could have been prevented.' He paused. 'I don't mean Stefan, of course.'

'I don't think we wasted too much time,' said Hanley abruptly. 'I may be overreacting about Chambers. He's a businessman, not a philanthropist, and the paper was losing readers.'

'So his campaigning journalist had to be muzzled.'

'Bennett was going too far,' Hanley admitted and Boyd guessed he'd been thinking through what he'd said to him.

'In what way?' he prompted.

'He'd begun condemning Seagate and its residents – rather than simply trying to educate them.' Hanley got up. 'Did you see my minder as you came in?'

Boyd realized he hadn't and hurried to the door, flinging it open. The plainclothes officer was sitting on a bench, watching the sea. He didn't turn round, and Boyd couldn't work out whether this was a good or bad sign.

'He's there now.'

'Are you saying he wasn't when you came in?' Hanley was obviously panic-stricken and Boyd felt a wave of irritation. Surely to God Hanley could be open with him now? He decided to get tough.

'Are you being threatened?'

'No.'

'Have you told me everything?'

'Of course.'

'Are you married?' asked Boyd suddenly.

'No. I was, but we divorced a couple of years ago.'

'Where's your wife now?'

'In London, with our daughter.'

'They're not being leant on?'

'No.'

'Then what is it?'

Hanley seemed indignant. 'Have you forgotten about the other killings? Surely I'm just as vulnerable.'

'Depending on what you know.'

'I've told you all I know.'

'You'd be a fool to hold out on me at this late stage. Is someone leaning on you?' Boyd was much more aggressive now.

'Absolutely not.'

'Do you know who killed Day and King?'

'Don't be a fool.'

'Look, you've got police protection. OK, so he disappeared for a few minutes, but maybe he wanted to check something out – so tell me why you're so worried.'

Boyd stared straight at Hanley and for a moment his hopes soared. There was something in Hanley's eyes that told him he was on the verge of confiding in him.

Then the moment passed.

'I'm going to get some lunch.'

'A table for two? You and your shadow?' Boyd laughed at the incongruous picture he had summoned up. But as Hanley shrugged on his coat and walked out, Boyd felt an eroding sense of inevitability.

Following Hanley out into the freezing air, he saw him walking slowly towards the town. A metre or so behind him was the plainclothes police officer, Hanley's protector. Both of them looked vulnerable. Leave it to the professionals, Boyd thought, as he went back into the office to phone Bennett.

'Carl Bennett.'

'My name's Rick James. I'm working for Seekers. I wonder if I could come and see you?'

'What about?' he said bluntly.

'I'd like to talk to you about the articles you wrote concerning the asylum seekers.'

'What for?'

'I admire what I've heard about you.'

'Who from?'

'Hanley.'

'I still don't know what you want,' he persisted, but Boyd thought he could detect more anxiety than dismissiveness in his tone.

'I've been invited to the Lorta shenanigans tomorrow,' Boyd said, knowing he sounded too jovial. 'I just need some background.'

Bennett sighed. 'Can you come round right away? I can give you half an hour. Then I've got to go out on a job.'

'I'll be with you in five minutes.'

Boyd put down the phone. Had Bennett really been anxious, or had he imagined it?

The orange orb of the winter sun hung limply over Seagate, bringing a golden light to the waves that crashed on to the pebble beach. Melting icicles hung everywhere – on the promenade shelters, the skating rink, the great hulk of the down-at-heel pier and the ornate public toilet, crenellated and columned, which dominated the lower seafront.

Boyd walked up the high street towards the centre of town. At least half the shops were boarded up and another department store, a grandiose Victorian building with towers, had been turned into a tatty indoor market, the once elegant shop windows steamed up and covered in cost-cutting adverts.

The *Seagate Observer* offices were next door, dwarfed by the department store and an art deco building that might once have been a cinema. The windows were full of neatly framed photographs of local events, all of which were suitably bland, none of them representing the asylum seekers in any shape or form. Grey photographs depicting a fete in the mayor's garden, schoolchildren lined up for sports activities, images of Seagate in all seasons, were on display as if there had been a cleansing, a total removal of the dread words 'asylum seeker'.

Boyd opened the smudged glass door and found himself in a reception area that clearly hadn't had a make-over since the sixties. Plastic was everywhere, even down to the long counter over which hung a neon sign that no longer worked, carrying the legend SEAGATE OBSERVER – SERVING THE COMMUNITY SINCE 1932.

Boyd rang a bell and a young woman emerged. 'Can I help you?'

'I've got an appointment with Carl Bennett.'

'I don't think he's in.' She sounded almost triumphant.

'I've got an appointment,' Boyd insisted.

'I'll see what I can do.' The tone of her voice implied there was very little she *could* do, but at least she picked up an internal telephone which rang for a long time before being answered. While the phone was ringing there was a pleased light of negativity in her eyes, and when the eventual response came she looked disappointed.

'Someone's here for you,' the receptionist snapped. She turned to Boyd, wrinkling her nose as if he had dog shit on his shoes. 'Name?'

'Rick James from Seekers.'

She gazed at him without interest and then returned to the phone, repeating the name and identification with a marked air of indifference. She listened and nodded.

'He'll see you,' she said reluctantly, putting down the phone.

'Where do I find him?'

'Take the lift to the second floor.' She yawned, retrieving a handbag from underneath the counter and pulling out a mirror, gazing into it as if surprised she still existed. Maybe we're all going to fade away soon, just like Seagate, thought Boyd as he hurried to the lift. First the town. Now its inhabitants.

Carl Bennett was standing outside the clanking, old-fashioned and iron-grilled lift. He was short and dapper, in a sports jacket and corduroy trousers, his round, pale face making him look younger than the early thirties Boyd guessed him to be.

'Mr James?'

'Yes.' They shook hands limply and Bennett took Boyd into a small overheated office.

Bennett sat behind a scratched wooden desk and waved Boyd to a chair beside him.

'Is this your office?' asked Boyd, looking round at the scarred walls and out-of-date printer's calender.

'This is an interview room.' Bennett's voice was more resonant than it had been on the phone. A broadcasting sort of voice, Boyd thought, noticing that Bennett had closed the door firmly behind him. 'I haven't much time,' he said, but the warning came across as defensive.

'I won't take up much of it. I just wanted to know why the *Observer* was no longer campaigning on behalf of the asylum seekers.'

'We're not against them.'

'But you used to give them a good deal of support.'

'That's not on. Not now.' Bennett paused. 'Apparently I was losing the paper circulation.' He sounded bitter, disaffected.

Boyd looked curiously at Bennett's boyish face and tousled fair hair. There was something familiar about his manner which he couldn't immediately identify. Then Boyd realized that, like Hanley, like most people he had met in Seagate, Bennett was afraid.

Boyd decided to capitalize on his anxiety and came straight to the point. 'The atmosphere in the town is very volatile, isn't it?'

'You can say that again.' Bennett spoke a little too excitedly. 'Of course it was volatile before the asylum seekers began to arrive in big numbers. Most people are on the dole. They resent that, and now of course the presence of the asylum seekers has worked them up even more.'

'That's not all, is it?'

'Well, of course there's the Roma Lorta visit, to say nothing of the serial killer and the robbery that ended in the little boy's death. It's all a bit much for a dead-end seaside resort.'

'And they say nothing happens in Seagate. In fact it's a reporter's dream,' said Boyd. 'You should do well out of it.'

Bennett had the grace to blush. It was a strange effect, making him look more schoolboyish than ever – but a schoolboy from another era. Jennings, perhaps.

'Yes. I have to agree,' said Bennett. 'It's hard to know which story to go for.'

'No doubt you've been feeding the London press.'

'Of course,' said Bennett crisply. 'And how about you, Mr James? Are you a volunteer or a paid-up member of staff at Seekers?'

'A member of staff. The second member of staff.'

Bennett nodded, and although Boyd knew he was probably far from satisfied he had no intention of filling him in with Rick James's full history. The story sounded less and less convincing every time he told it.

'So you wanted to pick my brains?' asked Bennett.

'I'm conscious of holding you up.'

'To hell with that. Have a good pick.'

'Thank you. I wanted your assessment of the asylum

seekers' general council – Mile Kropitz, Edina Milstein, Fitim Kadic and Josif Genzo.'

'I think they've joined together to settle old scores. Not necessarily to represent the asylum seekers,' said Bennett, and Boyd gazed at him in surprise.

'Any hard evidence?'

'Not a lot. But I'm sure I'm right.' Bennett picked up a newspaper from the floor behind the desk. 'What do you think of this? It's tomorrow's offering.'

The front page of the broadsheet was heavy with black type: POLICE ADVISE ALERT.

DI Faraday of Seagate CID warned residents of Seagate yesterday that a serial killer could be on the loose in the town. Councillor Harry Day, president of the refugee charity Seekers, was found dead, washed up on the beach on Thursday. Jack King, owner of Fantail Amusements and a prominent local businessman, was attacked that night and died of knife wounds to the chest.

DI Faraday commented, 'At the moment we are concentrating on Seagate itself in the belief that the killer may be in the locality and we would be grateful if members of the public would come forward with any information at all – however small.'

Further down the page was another headline: LORTA COMES TO SEAGATE.

There is rising concern that an assassination attempt may be made on Roma Lorta during his tour of the asylum-seeking population in the UK. Lorta was originally President of Lubic, the state that has once again plunged into ethnic cleansing. Both the US and UK governments are anxious to reinstate him. Lorta, as a strong Tito-like leader, would have a good chance of unifying his country.

As a result of the assassination scare, local police, aided by Special Branch officers, are to step up security.

Finally, in the bottom right-hand corner of the page, was a smaller headline: NO LEADS TO RAID.

So far Seagate CID have drawn a blank on the raid on the security truck outside HSBC in Audley Square last Monday. During the course of the raid, the getaway van skidded and killed

Stefan Kovac, originally from Kosovo. Ten-year-old Stefan lived with his mother, Rila Kovac, who is an asylum seeker.

'So you're printing three stories on the front page,' said Boyd.

'And getting the readers to make their own links.'

'You can't speculate.'

'As much as my career's worth at this stage,' agreed Bennett. 'Chambers would have no hesitation in blackening my name to everyone who matters. However, I don't reckon it'll be long before the three stories merge.'

'I gather you almost lost your job over your support of the asylum-seeker community.'

'Who told you that? Hanley?'

'And Edina Milstein.'

'She's a clever woman.' Bennett suddenly became less detached. 'And a real fount of wisdom in the community.' He paused and then continued. 'They're right. My boss couldn't take it any longer. As I said, we were losing circulation. He's not a bad guy, but all his investments are in Seagate. God help him.'

'*Would* he have sacked you?'

'Well, he hasn't so far. But I'm not hanging around to find out.'

'When you first started to support the asylum seekers, what were you hoping to achieve?' asked Boyd slowly.

'I was doing more than promoting tolerance. I was trying to get the readers to be curious. The English are the least curious race in the world. Here we have a large group of refugees with fascinating backgrounds, but naturally the residents only see them as enemies.'

'Maybe they've brought Seagate down even further,' suggested Boyd.

'Seagate's finished anyway. Anyone who has the slightest initiative should have got out a long time ago.'

'If you think the arrival of Lorta and the killings and the robbery are linked, how *would* you link them?' asked Boyd.

'An awful lot of people in Lubic don't want Lorta – not

at any price. He's seen as an American lackey and they want someone of their own. Lubic is an emerging state. They don't want to go back to a long-term holding operation – to another Tito.'

'Tito was his own man and he held the former Yugoslavia together very effectively,' said Boyd, trying to push Bennett into confrontation.

'That's all past history. Now each of the states has an identity of its own.'

'After a bloodbath.'

'And maybe more to come,' Bennett admitted.

'I wonder how long it will take to establish a solution that doesn't have to be UN patrolled?'

'A national identity that really works isn't easy to achieve. Not one that overrides cultural and religious differences.'

'You must have become an expert on the Balkans,' said Boyd.

'I have in a fractured sort of way.' Bennett was modest. 'And I know Lorta's not the right person for this job. At some time or other he'll have to go. But hopefully not in Seagate.'

'Do you reckon there's a real danger of that happening?'

'There seem to be indications. The robbery felt like fundraising to me. But whether they could bring it off is another matter. Sometimes the asylum seekers seem as vacuous as the denizens of Seagate.'

'Denizens.' Boyd repeated the word, relishing the sound. 'That's rather a good description.'

Bennett laughed, his boyish good looks accentuated. 'Expresses their grey anonymity, doesn't it? But in fact Lorta's visit is changing all that. The mass is splitting up into its component parts and the situation is becoming extremely volatile.'

'So you think there *will* be an assassination attempt?'

'I could be wrong, but everything seems to point that way. Hard to say whether they'll handle it themselves or recruit local labour. But if my fund-raising theory's correct it's almost certainly the latter.'

That's where I come in, thought Boyd. The shadowy figure in the middle, set up as a conduit. Then he remembered the spinning tyres of the getaway vehicle, the inability to control the van, the thud, the child's body flying into the grey snow.

'Are you OK?' asked Bennett.

'Just tired. I've been packing a lot in.'

'You must be very committed.'

'I am. I want to make a difference.' Boyd winced as the cliché sprang off his tongue.

They looked at each other. Boyd had the idea that Bennett was wincing too.

He tried another tack by coming cleaner – within his scenario at least. 'Actually, I've been inside.'

'What for?'

'Credit card fraud.'

'Anything else?'

'Isn't that enough?'

'So joining Seekers is an attempt at restitution?'

'I don't have to tell you all this.' Boyd was irritated.

'You must forgive me. I'm naturally curious.'

'That's OK.' Boyd knew that if Rick James was going to survive he had to learn to cope with this sort of reaction. 'Anyway, I knew I had to turn myself round.'

'As a sort of social worker.'

'To see if I could live in an unfriendly place and embrace an unpopular cause.'

'How have you found it?'

'Not as unfriendly as I'd expected.'

'Have you met the central council?'

'Briefly. My main contact has been Edina Milstein.'

'Do you fancy her?' The question hung in the air for a shade too long.

'As a matter of fact I do.' Boyd suddenly realized that he did.

142

Bennett laughed. 'Same here. There's something about her.'

'What's that for you?' asked Boyd.

'She's determined. I always fancy determined women. And you?'

'Hard to pin the attraction down.'

'Kept well under control, is it? A little bird told me you were a born-again Christian.'

Boyd made a rapid decision. 'Maybe I was.'

'You mean you aren't any longer?'

'It was something I went through. A sort of cleaning out the stables job. But I think it's over now.'

'That's an interesting way of looking at religion.'

'I find it depressing,' said Boyd. 'Nothing lasts.'

'You can't be a born-again Christian on your own. You need to tune in to a local bunch of happy-clappies.'

'I don't think so,' said Boyd and returned them firmly to the agenda. 'Are you seriously telling me there could be an attempt on Lorta's life tomorrow? And, if so, it could be by a local criminal hired by the asylum seekers?'

'There's an irony in that, I admit.'

'You may well be right, though,' said Boyd. He paused and then asked, 'And the serial killer?'

'Practice makes perfect?' suggested Bennett.

'You really think the serial killer was limbering up?' Boyd sounded incredulous.

'I don't know.' Bennett's voice was flat and Boyd looked at him with a new interest, quick to identify that under the professional journalist was a frightened man. Just like Hanley. Or was he reading too much into it all?

'I'm shit scared,' said Bennett, confirming Boyd's suspicions.

'No wonder.' Boyd deliberately fed his anxiety. 'You can always get out,' he added.

'Not while the story's coming to the boil.'

'You'd risk your life for that?'

'My career's at stake.'

'So even if you can't write for the *Observer*, then you'll write for the nationals.'

'If things come to a head, everyone'll want the story.'

'And you're ambitious enough to hang around?'

'All part of the job.' Bennett tried to sound casual.

'You could go to Faraday and get protection. Hanley has.'

'Hanley might be seen as a rather worthier case.'

'I'm not so sure about that,' said Boyd.

Boyd decided to return to Seekers and think. He needed to sift fact from theory.

As he walked down the promenade in the pale winter light, the town seemed to close in on him, hostile and threatening, and the sea, to Boyd always a symbol of escape, had retreated to the horizon, exposing mud and icy rock pools. The shingle was still covered in snow as if the melt had been put on hold.

As he reached the office he could see a long queue of asylum seekers waiting patiently by the phone box, phone cards in hand, displaced persons, waiting in limbo to phone a near mythical home. They were dressed in dun colours and exuded an air of Central European poverty that Boyd had once witnessed on a visit to Poland. There was no expression on their faces and only their children seemed alert, looking longingly over the pebble beach at the long reaches of sand – as if they hoped the distant ocean would roll back even further and they could walk home over the mud and sand, wearing rucksacks and carrying suitcases.

Boyd hurried across the road and unlocked the door to the office. Once inside he sat down in the chair beside Hanley's desk, the place where he usually sat, originally as Rick James and now as Daniel Boyd.

His head ached and Boyd closed his eyes – and quickly opened them again. All he could see in his mind's eye was the interior of the Grand Hotel and, in particular, Edina's flat. So Bennett felt the same.

The phone rang.

Boyd picked up the receiver, sweating in spite of the cold.

Hanley was in a phone booth, his voice crackling like the ice on the foreshore.

'Rick?' It was the first time anyone had used the given name of Boyd's alias and for a moment he wondered who Hanley wanted. Then he pulled himself together. Hanley was only being careful in case the phone was being tapped.

'Mr Hanley?'

'Yes. I've had some thoughts I'd like to discuss. Can you meet me?'

'Where?'

'I'm in a call box by the station. I forgot my mobile. I left it in my desk drawer. Can you bring it with you?'

'Of course.'

'Make it quick!' Hanley's voice suddenly sounded panicky.

'I'll be there in a few minutes.'

'Be here faster than that,' Hanley pleaded.

'Is something wrong?'

There was no reply.

But Boyd was too late. The crowd was already there, surrounding the telephone box, and he could hear the sound of sirens closing in. Pushing his way to the front, Boyd saw Hanley's body lying half in and half out of the kiosk. He had fallen on his back and his head had been almost severed.

Boyd shook. The shock waves flooded him and then he felt someone grab his arm.

Turning apprehensively, Boyd saw DI Faraday beside him. 'Not another one.'

'It's out of control,' muttered Boyd.

145

'Bloody asylum seekers.'

'Why blame them?'

'Why not? It's obvious, isn't it?'

'Why kill a councillor, a businessman and a charity worker?'

'Maybe they're making a protest.' Faraday was dogged.

'What about?'

'Their plight. Let's take a look.'

They both moved forward and stared down at Hanley. There was blood, but surprisingly little of it. Then he saw the deep mark of the wire that was still in place around Hanley's neck.

'He's been garotted,' said Faraday. 'One drowned, another stabbed and this time a garotting. This killer's versatile.' Faraday had been half-whispering, but now he said in a louder tone, 'And you'll be able to officially identify him, Mr James?'

I could be a suspect, thought Boyd wildly. A prison sentence, a conversion and a mission. His alias could tell against him now. Then he realized he was simply panicking. Faraday knew exactly who he was.

'Yes,' he said. 'That's Hanley . . .'

They both gazed down at him as the pathologist arrived. Then Faraday drew Boyd aside and, taking his arm, led him towards the unmarked police vehicle.

Once in the front passenger seat of Faraday's car, Boyd said, 'He'd just phoned me.'

'Where from?'

'There – that box outside the station. He'd forgotten his mobile. I've brought it with me.'

'Any messages?'

Boyd cursed himself. Why hadn't he checked Hanley's mobile? He punched at the buttons and received the information that there was one saved message.

It was short and to the point. The voice had no accent and sounded muffled. 'I think this should stop. There is a way. Meet me at the station. At the telephone box opposite the entrance.'

When the message was finished they played it back several times. 'Effectively disguised,' said Faraday rather unnecessarily.

'The killings have to be connected,' said Boyd. 'Although the victims aren't.'

'I disagree.'

'You mean they were all involved with asylum seekers?'

'Got it in one,' said Faraday impatiently.

They were silent, watching the crowd being pushed back by a couple of police officers while the paramedics began to wrap Hanley's corpse in a body bag.

'Do you really think someone in the asylum-seeker community is killing Seagate's citizens?'

'I don't know. But in three days we've got three deaths,' said Faraday. 'That's pretty good going.'

'Are you going to let Lorta's visit go ahead?'

'Definitely.'

'Why?'

'It'll bring the situation to a head. We've got Special Branch, Lorta bodyguards and a large police presence. Officers are being drafted in from all over the county.'

'Wait a minute,' said Boyd. 'Let's just suppose the killings have nothing to do with Lorta. Why these three men?'

'I think they *are* to do with Lorta and they were targeted. Take Day. He was a Labour councillor. And president of Seekers.'

'So that singles him out?'

'He could have been seen as criminally ineffective. Representing an offensive attempt by the government to evade responsibility and put aid in the hands of amateurs.' Faraday warmed to his theme. 'Maybe someone wanted Lorta's attention drawn to that.'

'What about King?'

'He had a finger on the pulse of the villains in Seagate, and he made it very clear he wasn't keen on refugees. Flip the coin and see him as a plant, reporting back on what he sees and hears. Maybe he knew too much about the plans for Lorta's reception. After all, he was an informer.'

'Was he any use?' asked Boyd.

'Not a lot. But he should have been.'

'You reckon he was holding stuff back?'

'Possibly.'

'Are you?'

'Now why should I do that?' Faraday was defensive. 'We're meant to be working together.'

Boyd looked sceptical. 'And Hanley, of course, fits into the Seekers connection,' he conceded. 'But he was another police informer –'

'Another angle might be the revenge factor,' said Faraday.

'Revenge on Seagate? By the asylum seekers?' Boyd scoffed. 'That seems a very long shot.'

'But can't be ruled out. There's a lot of hostility on their side too, according to Hanley.'

'Was *his* information any use?'

'Yes, but not a lot better than King's. There was never anything really solid to go on.' Faraday paused. 'I know you were very put out to find two men already in operation on your patch, but they were only informers. You're different. And Creighton tells me you're very experienced.'

'I haven't contributed anything so far. Events have moved so fast I haven't even had time to take a broad look at the situation. Day seems to be the odd man out whichever way you look at it though. He's not an obvious target for the Seagate criminal classes and he was trying to *help* the asylum seekers. I suppose that they were all three quite prominent in the Seagate community. That could have been enough. But somehow I don't think so. I can't get away from the feeling that Lorta's visit is the key, and we've only got twenty-four hours. Are you sure you shouldn't cancel his visit? It's all very well to talk about allowing the situation to come to a head, but heads'll roll if there are any more casualties.'

'We've got to take the risk,' said Faraday stubbornly, but Boyd shook his head.

'Three men are dead,' he muttered. 'Why ask for more?' He paused. 'Not to mention my contribution.'

'Look – I know how you feel about killing that child. It was an accident. You've got to put it behind you.'

'You think it's interfering with my work?' said Boyd, unable to conceal his bitter resentment.

'Yes,' said Faraday baldly.

'Have you spoken to Creighton?'

'He thinks the same.'

'So what is he going to do? Pull me off the case?'

'No. It's too late for that. Look, Boyd, we've got twenty-four hours. For God's sake, get your act together.'

Boyd was silent. 'Maybe I should come off the damn case. I'm not making any impact.'

'It's too late to walk off the territory.' Faraday was obviously regretting his criticisms and was almost pleading now. 'My fucking job's on the line, and so is yours. I very much care about losing mine – even if you don't.'

Boyd stared at Faraday blankly, wondering for the hundredth time what he did want to do with his life. Where would he be without an alias to bury himself in?

'I'll go and see the council of asylum seekers again, try and suss them out. Maybe one of them – or all of them – has a finger on the trigger.'

'Unlikely,' said Faraday smugly, returning to his natural habit of needling Boyd. 'But they may know something they're misguidedly trying to handle themselves.'

Boyd reached for the door handle and saw that the police had cordoned off the telephone kiosk with tape. The media had arrived and there was a television crew. He let go of the handle.

'For God's sake get stuck in on that council, Boyd. Time's running right out.'

'It would be much simpler to stop the visit.' Boyd tried a last ditch stand.

'It wouldn't be simple at all. Just aim to bring things to

a head *before* Lorta arrives.' Faraday was insistent. 'After all, that's your job.'

'And what about the TV crew?'

'Don't talk to them. I'm going to do that.'

Boyd opened the door and had a microphone thrust into his face. 'What are the police going to do next?' asked a young woman. 'This is the third killing in three days.'

'I'm not a police officer,' said Boyd. 'Just a witness. I can't talk to you.'

He hurried past her, just in time to hear Faraday say, 'I don't want to make any comment at the moment, but I can assure you that we're confident of making an arrest very soon.'

'Is the killer an asylum seeker?' asked the reporter.

'No comment.'

'Are you going to allow Lorta to speak in Seagate?' she asked. 'After all that's happened, surely it's too dangerous for him to take a risk like that?'

'I'm afraid I can't say any more,' Boyd heard Faraday saying, but the reporter kept asking questions. He suddenly felt sorry for Faraday. Just a little bit.

Boyd knew that he had to work fast. As he walked through the cold streets to the Grand he let his mind sift once again through everything he knew about the case.

Slowly he became increasingly convinced that Day, King and Hanley had been killed because they knew too much about the assassination attempt. Was it a name? A means? A plan?

Now he was treading warily across Audley Square. Despite the slow thaw, the ice seemed worse here than anywhere and he almost tripped over a couple of times. Then he realized he had taken the route he always avoided. The route that would take him past Stefan's flowers. Now he was almost on top of them. Where were they? He saw no sign of the heaped-up pile of flowers at all. Then Boyd saw a mound of snow: a passing car must have spattered them with slush which had frozen solid. He squatted down and began to scrape away the snow. The wind was bitingly cold and he had to use a steel pocket comb to whittle away at the ice until he slowly uncovered the flowers. He found the task had given him both pain and satisfaction. He worked on for a while longer, gazing up at the pock-marked face of the Grand, trying to work out which was Edina's bedroom.

'Forty-forty,' said the voice and Boyd looked up to see Arthur, with his football raised in his right hand. He had never looked closely at him before and now saw that he was quite young, maybe in his early thirties, clean-shaven with blue eyes. But it was the eyes that disturbed him the most. They were fixed on a point somewhere above Boyd's head and they had no expression in them at all. For a moment he wondered if the man was blind and then dismissed the idea.

'I've seen you before,' said Boyd, getting up and going over to stand beside him. But there was no hint of any expression on Arthur's face; it was as if he had drawn on a mask.

'Forty-forty.'

'What does that mean?'

'Forty-forty.'

'What do you think about the murders that have taken place in the town?'

Arthur said nothing.

'Do you think there's a serial killer here?'

'It's me,' said Arthur, turning away and raising the football as far as he could in his right hand. 'No one cares.' He began to walk stiffly away.

Boyd hurried after him and grabbed his arm. He was surprised to feel solid muscle. But then if he had lifted a football so many times above his head . . .

'Why did you kill them?'

'They were wrong,' said Arthur, not attempting to pull away.

151

'What do you mean, wrong?'

'They didn't fit.'

'Into what?'

'The box.' Arthur then pulled himself away and began to hurry down the street.

Boyd sighed and squatted down again to resume scraping the snow off the flowers. If only life could be so simple. A madman did it. So we're all off the hook.

'You're doing a good job,' said a voice and Boyd was startled to see Carl Bennett, wearing a jerkin and jeans.

'It seemed a shame . . .'

'I agree. Where were you going?'

'I've got an appointment.'

'OK. I was going to ask you if you'd like a drink.'

'Another time,' said Boyd. 'Where are *you* going?'

'Out for a walk and a think. I would imagine we're both thinking the same thing. Why kill them?'

'Yes. And it must be because they knew about something – or someone.' For the second time, Boyd got to his feet.

'Connected with a possible assassination of Lorta.'

'Why else take such a risk?'

'Maybe someone's simply trying to stop the visit.'

'Too high a risk for that, I reckon. The only way to test that one out would be to cancel it.'

'They won't do that,' replied Bennett. 'They'll just draft in extra security. The government's anxious to ensure that Lorta is seen and believed. And you reckon there'll be an attempt on his life?'

'In my opinion the indications all point to that,' said Boyd. 'They knew something or someone important – all three of them.'

'But I still don't think they'll cancel Lorta.'

'It seems madness not to.' Boyd paused and then added, 'Unless the government *wants* him dead.'

'It's not in their interest,' said Bennett. 'You're only being devil's advocate.'

'It's a role that suits me.' Boyd began to walk away.

'Is it nosy if I ask you about the visit you're making? It wouldn't be to Edina Milstein by any chance?'

'How *did* you guess?' Boyd hurried across the square and nearly slipped again.

'Careful how you go,' Bennett advised him. 'You may not have noticed, but Seagate's become rather a treacherous place lately.'

'I'm glad you've come back,' said Edina. 'I need a – what is it you say? – another party?'

'A third party,' suggested Boyd.

'I've got something to show you.'

'What is it?'

'I found some things.'

'What are they? How do you mean, you found them?'

'Put it like this, someone told me about them, but I can't reveal who.'

'Another third party?' asked Boyd.

'If you like.'

'This is no good. You have to tell me more.'

She was sitting on the sofa in jeans and a tight-fitting top and Boyd felt an overwhelming surge of desire for her.

'I can't. But you have to come and see.' She got up.

'Where are we going?'

'To Dream World,' she said. 'Someone has to take the responsibility. Please help me.'

Deeply intrigued and more than a little fearful, Boyd was forced to say he would.

Chapter Fifteen

Boyd followed Edina Milstein out of the Grand Hotel and down the street. She walked fast and he had difficulty keeping up. Occasionally she exchanged subdued greetings with friends, but she never slowed her pace for a minute and Boyd was envious of her sure-footedness on the ice.

'Slow down,' he pleaded. 'This black ice is dangerous.' But not nearly as dangerous as Seagate, Boyd thought as he remembered Bennett's words.

Boyd saw an old couple shovelling snow off their front path by the light of a street lamp. They turned to stare at Edina and then muttered something to each other that Boyd was sure was derogatory. How many of Seagate's residents regarded the asylum seekers with loathing, he wondered. For many they were like aliens, living amongst them but not with them. A world within a world.

And what was the attitude of the asylum seekers themselves? Did they regard the population of Seagate as a solid wall of discrimination and view them with suspicion and hostility? Did they feel a disenfranchised people, facing another less dangerous but chillingly uncaring closed community?

Now they were walking down a narrow side street between the bus station and a warehouse. At the end was a steel gate, its surface badly dented, as if something large and heavy had backed into it.

Checking round to see that she was not being observed,

Edina climbed athletically over the gate and signalled Boyd to follow.

He clambered over as fast as he could, but missed his footing on the other side and almost fell. Edina discreetly looked away, but Boyd felt humiliated.

'We're in the amusement park,' she said. 'But like everything else around here it's in ruins.'

They turned a corner and found themselves behind a heavily vandalized children's roundabout. Once the horses had been brightly painted. Now they were covered in graffiti and some of their heads had been hacked off.

Emerging from the shadow of the roundabout Boyd saw dereliction on every side. Dream World had been completely wrecked.

'God, what a mess!'

'It reminds me of the Balkans,' said Edina sadly. 'I often come in here and think about it all. Sometimes I come out very angry; other times defensive – but occasionally I feel happy, as if I'm closer to my people.'

The lake, which might once have been the sparkling hub of Dream World, was full of old tyres, floating gently in circles. Grouped around the shores were a roller coaster, a dodgem track, a tower that contained a huge slide, a ghost train ride and a House of Horror, all badly damaged.

Boyd was considerably shocked. 'How long's the park been closed?'

'Only a few months.'

Edina sat down on the scarred wood of the dodgem track and Boyd joined her.

'You really come here to think?'

'Why not?'

'Isn't it dangerous?'

'For me to be here alone? Well, I usually sit in the old shooting range down there. That way I can see and not be seen.'

'Who do you watch?'

'The youth of your country. They come here to vandalize

the place. And there's a beaten-up old wreck of a car they can start up. See – down there by the lake.'

Boyd followed her gaze and saw a shapeless mass in the falling darkness.

'They keep crashing into things,' she said with a bitter smile. 'They never get tired of doing that. It seems to absorb them completely.'

'I still think it's dangerous for you to come down here alone,' said Boyd.

'Yes.' There was no trace of humour in her voice now. 'You would think that.'

'What do you mean?'

'You think small. All you British think small.'

Suddenly she was hostile and Boyd froze, the desire for her almost overcoming him.

'Like war? Like being an asylum seeker?'

'Now you're patronizing me.'

'Hardly.'

'It's true. That's why Seekers was founded. To patronize us. You English – you love to patronize.'

'Could that be confused with wanting to help you?' asked Boyd.

'What do you do? Fuck all!'

'Shut up!' said Boyd. Were they playing a game? A sexual game?

Suddenly Edina slapped him round the face and Boyd stood up, looking down at her.

'I'm sorry,' she said. 'Actually, I'm not sorry.'

'Make up your mind.'

But her temper had evaporated. Instead she seemed genuinely embarrassed. 'So a born-again Christian won't hit back.'

'I'm not sure that I'm as committed as I thought I was, but I still wouldn't want to hit you.'

'What do you mean?'

'God was a crutch when I came out of prison. But since I've been working at Seekers I've found him something of a liability.'

'Why?'

'It's not how the world works. I was giving myself a quick fix of idealism.'

'I don't see it that way. I believe in God.'

'After all you've been through?' Boyd was incredulous.

'I believe even more.'

'Why?'

'I survived, didn't I? And I'm going to survive here too. And so will Roma Lorta.'

'You believe in him too?'

'He's essential. To reunite Lubic.'

'But a lot of asylum seekers hate him.'

'That's why I need your help.'

'How?'

'I found something. I found something I shouldn't have found.'

'What's that?'

'As I said, I'll show you. But first of all I apologize for losing my temper.'

Edina went over to the coconut shy. At the back was a wooden screen. She bent down and pulled at the base of the screen, revealing a dim, dark space underneath. With some difficulty she dragged out a couple of Kalashnikovs, some ammunition and what looked to Boyd like plastic explosive.

'Christ! How did you find this?'

'I told you. Someone tipped me off. So I watched every evening and eventually saw someone come here and check these weapons were in place.'

'Did you recognize this person?'

'A tall man with dark hair. But I'd never seen him before.'

'Nationality?'

'British.'

'Are you sure?'

'He wasn't one of our people.'

'That doesn't make him British.'

157

'I'm afraid it does. Someone else joined him. They were talking in English.'

'I see.' Boyd tried to stop interrogating her. 'What do you want me to do about this?'

'Call the police.'

'Why didn't you?'

'Because they would suspect me. They would assume there had been a dispute – that I wanted to take revenge on someone.'

Boyd nodded. 'And you're quite sure they didn't see you?'

'I told you, I'm a survivor. I know how to handle things. They didn't see me.'

'So you've hung on to this information and done nothing.'

'I waited for you because I knew you'd help.'

'Why didn't you ring me at Seekers?'

'I couldn't take the risk.' She was getting angry again.

'OK. I'll call the police on my mobile.'

'Now?'

'Why not?'

'I don't want to be around. I'm very afraid of getting involved.'

'So where are you going?'

'Back to the Grand. Where else have I got to go?'

'The police'll want to talk to you.'

'I realize that.'

'So why not stay around?' asked Boyd.

'No.' Edina began to walk away from him. She didn't look back.

Boyd dialled Seagate Police Station and asked for Faraday. Fortunately, he was put through right away.

'I've found some weapons and explosives.' Boyd felt the adrenalin taking him over. At last he could surprise Faraday.

'How did you do that?' He sounded almost querulous.

'Edina Milstein showed me. Apparently she often gets into Dream World to – to reflect.'

'That's private property.'

'Mainly demolished by vandals,' said Boyd. 'I don't think it's that private any more.'

'I'm coming over. How did you get in?'

'Over the security gate.'

'Wait there. I'll be with you in a few minutes.'

Faraday arrived alone in an unmarked car. He got out, climbed the gate and joined Boyd.

'Show me.'

They walked over to the coconut shy and Boyd stood back.

Faraday gazed down at the rifles, the ammunition and the plastic explosives.

'She saw a man checking out the arsenal,' explained Boyd. 'Then he was joined by someone else. Milstein couldn't identify either of them. She's sure they were English.'

'She would be.' Faraday wasn't impressed.

'I'm sure she confided in me because she's afraid. Very afraid.'

'Of what her own people are doing?' suggested Faraday.

Boyd was silent.

Faraday shrugged. 'It seems a bit too easy, doesn't it? Edina Milstein trespasses and watches men she claims are English checking out a cache of weapons and explosives. So she gives them away. I suspect there are other motives. Surely you don't accept her story just like that?'

'Not without investigation.'

'That's a relief then. I'm going to have this stuff removed on the quiet. I don't want the media in on this. Particularly Carl Bennett. He'll stir the shit.' Faraday paused. 'Will Milstein tell him?'

'She might,' said Boyd.

'Then get over to the Grand and tell her to shut it.'

'You're going to have the stuff forensically –'

'Don't tell me what to do,' snapped Faraday.

Boyd was furious. Faraday was treating him like an errand boy. But it would be undignified to argue, so Boyd clambered over the gate again, cursing not just Faraday but Edina Milstein as well.

He glanced at his watch. It was just after eight and he was beginning to feel hungry and in desperate need of a drink, but he had to see Edina first.

Tramping the slush to the Grand, Boyd was increasingly sure that he was on the edge of a chasm. Should he speak to Creighton? Try yet again to get the Lorta visit cancelled? Or would Creighton take Faraday's side, also hoping to bring the situation to a head?

'Yes?' Edina sounded tired.

'Rick James.'

'I'll unlock.' Edina looked drawn. As soon as he was inside, she went and sat down on the couch. 'The police came?'

'Yes. DI Faraday. They're going to take the weapons back to the police station and let the forensic people check them out.'

'Fingerprints?'

'I don't know. I wiped yours,' said Boyd, drawing up a chair opposite her. 'Faraday asked me to stress that he didn't want the media involved.'

'I haven't spoken to anyone.'

'Your own people?'

'Not even to them. I suppose this Faraday man doesn't believe anything I told you.'

'He didn't go along with them being British. He seemed to prefer them not to be.'

Edina gave a weak laugh. 'I'm sorry I got you involved now.'

'I can't stay long,' he said, knowing that if he did he'd do something wrong. Wrong for them both.

'Why not?'

'I'm exhausted. I need to sleep.'

'You can sleep here.'

Boyd gazed back at her in astonishment, wondering if the attraction could be mutual.

'You can lie on the bed. I won't trouble you.'

Was she deliberately winding him up? He looked at her closely and had the impression she was afraid. Was *that* why she wanted him to stay?

'What are you afraid of?' he challenged her.

'I don't understand.'

'Who are you afraid of then?'

'That's a ridiculous question.' She wouldn't make eye contact.

'Is it? You can tell me, you know.'

She glanced at him quickly and for a moment he thought he saw relief in her eyes. Was she going to tell him?

'I'm not afraid of anyone, Mr James. Not even you.'

'Why should you be afraid of me?' She didn't reply and there was an uneasy silence. 'Are the arrangements for the Lorta visit all sewn up?' asked Boyd awkwardly.

'I'm sure they are.'

'It seems that Faraday is going to let the visit go ahead – although I'm sure he could still be overruled by Special Branch.'

'What is the likelihood of them interfering?' For the first time she seemed more got together.

'I don't know. I've no experience of these things, but the cache of weapons is obviously worrying. There could be more and they could be used.'

'It would be terrible if Lorta's visit was cancelled.'

'Why?' asked Boyd, needing to be devil's advocate.

'He could give people hope.' Edina suddenly got to her feet. 'If you're so tired, Mr James, I suggest you go home to bed.'

Boyd gazed at her resentfully. She *was* only playing games, he thought. 'One last thing,' he said crisply, determined not to let her see she'd scored. '*Can* Seekers be represented tomorrow? If the visit goes ahead?'

'I asked the others. Mile was not so pleased, but Fitim

and Josif agreed. And now that Hanley is dead, you *are* Seekers. What's the expression? You are a one-man band.'

'I shall have to wait for Mrs Browning. See what she says.'

'She is the Member of Parliament?'

'She used to be.'

'Well, that's your problem, Mr James. Now we're both exhausted and I must prepare for tomorrow.'

'Are you making a speech?'

'A few words of introduction.'

'I'm sure you'll do that very well.'

'I think I will.'

Boyd went to the door and they shook hands.

Immediately he was outside in the corridor, Boyd felt a wave of frustration – on all levels. It was impossible to make Edina out and he wondered what she had been like before her life had been blown apart. Then he wondered what he'd been like.

Boyd met Rila Kovac as he came out of the lift. She was alone in the foyer, staring at nothing in particular.

He had dreaded another encounter. Now here it was – just when his spirits were at their lowest.

'Rila?'

'What is it?'

'Did you cash your cheque?'

'The funeral was paid for.'

'By –'

'Our people.'

'It's always the worst time,' he said.

'When?'

'After the arrangements are over. When there are no more arrangements to make. When there's just time to fill.'

'I've been filling up time for a long while. But there was always Stefan.' Rila's voice ended on a sob and Boyd,

162

standing over her, put an awkward arm around her shoulders.

'Do you need anything?'

'Yes.'

'Can I –'

'I want Stefan. I want him back.'

Boyd lay on his bed, mobile in hand, talking to Creighton.

'The visit's definitely going ahead,' said Creighton.

'Despite what I found?'

'Yes. There's no point in cancellation. We have full security. What we don't want to do is spread alarm. Lorta has to go back to Lubic and hold the place together.'

'Are you really expecting another Tito?'

'No. But we need stability – even if it's temporary.'

'What about the arms?'

'I'm not so concerned about them. I have a feeling they're a set-up.'

'To make us cancel?'

'Maybe.' Creighton seemed vague.

'And what about Milstein?'

'What about her?'

'I think she's on the level – except that I reckon the two guys who were checking over the weapons cache weren't English. I think it's more likely they were her own people – or some other group of asylum seekers.'

'How does that follow?'

'To hire a person – or persons – unknown, to attempt the assassination of Lorta, seems a really complicated idea. They would have to be paid. They would have to be reliable. They're more likely to keep it in the family.'

Creighton wasn't impressed. 'But our original theory was that the criminal element in Seagate *could* be involved. Surely the asylum seekers trying to protect Lorta would discover the identity of an assassin amongst their own community much more easily than someone from outside.

For God's sake – that was why we set up that disastrous robbery in the first place.'

'So you're backing Milstein's story?'

'I'm not backing anyone's story. Nothing is what it seems; everything needs careful analysis. Look, tell me frankly, do you want to come off this job?' Creighton sounded weary.

'What makes you ask?'

'I don't think you've survived the accident, the death of the child. It's all too near to what happened – to your family. Look, Danny, I respect your judgement, and always have. But in this case –'

'You think I've lost it.'

'I think I should pull you out on compassionate grounds.'

'I don't want that to happen.'

'And there's something else. Edina Milstein.'

'Yes?'

'Are you being unprofessional?'

'Meaning am I screwing her?'

'Tell me the truth,' said Creighton gently.

'The truth is I haven't touched her.'

'OK,' said Creighton and Boyd wondered if he believed him.

'I realise I made a terrible error at the beginning, but no one was to know that. I may not have been one hundred per cent effective, but I don't think that would have undermined the master plan. The fact is – no one has contacted me.'

'It's early days,' said Creighton.

'Early days with time running out. I don't want to be pulled off this job. That would make what I did so much worse.'

'As long as you reassure me you don't have to be pulled off Milstein.'

'That's cheap.'

'You're an undercover police officer. Nothing's cheap.' Creighton paused and Boyd could feel him assessing the

164

situation. Then he said, 'Open your eyes, open your mind. I'll give you until Lorta's gone. But if I find that child is still affecting your judgement I'm going to have to pull you. And we won't be having this discussion again.'

'I certainly hope not.' Boyd knew he sounded ungracious.

'Are you officially attending the Lorta event?'

'As a representative – now the only representative – of Seekers. Yes.'

'The place will have to be checked out by Special Branch.'

'Let's hope they're up to it,' said Boyd bitterly. 'Even if I'm not.'

He put the phone down before Creighton could reply.

Boyd's mobile rang a few moments later and he picked it up wearily, wondering if Creighton had changed his mind.

'Mr James?'

'Yes.'

'This is Hilary Browning. I wanted to give you a ring to thank you for carrying on in the face of adversity.'

'I intend to try.'

'Losing Day and Hanley in this appalling way – I just don't know what to say to you. Have the police *any* ideas?'

'Have you spoken to Faraday?'

'Too many times.'

'And?'

'He just shuts me up. Keeps telling me enquiries are being pursued. Do you have any thoughts?'

'None. I'm as shocked as you are. The fact that these good men were murdered beggars belief.' Boyd had often wanted to use the phrase. There was something definitive about it.

'I agree. But do you think the police have any leads?'

'I just don't know,' said Boyd. 'They're as evasive with me as they are with you.'

'Will you be attending the Lorta meeting?'

'Yes. Apparently there's going to be very tight security.'

'You think it's tight enough?'

'As far as I know.'

'I shall be coming along.'

'We need to be represented. I'm sure the charity needs to survive.'

'I'll make it my business to see that it does,' said Hilary Browning. 'You can be sure of that.'

But when Boyd had put the phone down, he knew he couldn't be sure of anything.

Chapter Sixteen

The ballroom of the Grand Hotel had received a short-term make-over. Cheap rush matting covered the damaged carpet while the wall above the stage had been hung with coloured sheets that concealed the damp stains. Canvas chairs had been hired and some pot plants had been scattered about, but nothing could really disguise the old ballroom's air of neglect and decay.

Boyd sat down at the table which had been reserved for him at the foot of the stage. He scattered some leaflets about the aims and objectives of Seekers on its scarred surface and tried to look purposeful, but inside he felt increasingly anxious and claustrophobic.

The canvas chairs were largely taken up by asylum seekers, men, women and children, all with the muted expression on their faces that Boyd had come to recognize as the hallmark of not only past misery but present apprehension. He noticed particularly a boy in cheap corduroy trousers and a torn sweater, staring into space, his thoughts clearly elsewhere, hands clasping and unclasping on his lap.

Hilary Browning, in an enormous tent-like coat with a hood, was sitting on her own at the back near the door through which Lorta and his entourage would eventually emerge. Boyd wondered whether she would come and join him at the Seekers' table, but had to admit he was relieved when she didn't.

Uniformed police officers stood round the sides of the ballroom, a group of them concentrated at the rear of the

167

stage. Boyd counted over a hundred and he wondered if they were armed, knowing they'd be useless if they weren't.

A central aisle had been cleared and the large police presence was enhanced by a number of youngish men in good suits, all too obviously belonging to Special Branch.

The council were already in position on the stage. Edina Milstein was talking to Mile Kropitz while Fitim Kadric and Josif Genzo seemed to be studiously ignoring them. There was a lectern with a microphone just to their right where Roma Lorta was going to give his address.

Boyd could feel the tension mounting. He glanced at Mile and Edina, wondering what they were talking about so vehemently. He noticed they were trying to keep what seemed to be an argument as unobtrusive as possible, frequently looking around them and then lowering their voices.

Finally, Mile walked away, hurrying down the steps, while Edina followed, pausing at Boyd's table.

'What's going on?' he whispered.

'Lorta will be here in a few minutes. I can't talk now.' But he could see she was desperate to talk. 'Mile is very angry with me,' she whispered.

'Why?'

'He accused me of withholding information. He would have preferred that I'd gone to him about the weapons cache.'

'Maybe you should have,' said Boyd slowly, and suddenly wondered why she hadn't.

'Mile feels we should have acted together.'

'Why didn't you?'

'This is not the place to talk. Lorta will be here any moment,' she repeated.

'Just tell me – why *did* you come to me?'

'Because I don't trust my colleagues,' she admitted.

'Why?'

'We are all so opposed in our views. For instance, they

168

can't even agree that Lorta should take power. They all have their own theories about what should be done. I thought I'd found someone who was objective.'

'You trusted me? You know them so much better. Why me?'

'I took a risk.'

'Isn't that what Kropitz is accusing you of?'

For once Edina seemed nonplussed. Boyd had never seen her like this before and was moved by her sudden and unexpected helplessness.

'In part.'

'I need to ask you a question.'

'Not here.'

'Very quickly.' Boyd knew he had to seize the moment. 'Are you sure those two men – the ones who were checking out the cache – really were English?'

'I heard them talking.'

'At that distance?'

'For God's sake – are you accusing me too? Why don't you stick to your charity work, Mr James? Isn't that what you're best at?'

'It's not as straightforward as that. The situation's volatile.'

'Are you going to back off?' She turned away from him, and as she began to climb up to the stage again Boyd watched her closely. There was something in her demeanour that he hadn't seen before. Why was she suddenly so afraid? Or was he making another mistake? Maybe her agitation was simply due to the rigours of the day.

Edina Milstein stood at the podium and raised a hand. There was a slow hush. In it, Boyd suddenly became aware of a large black spider swinging on a gossamer thread that was attached to a thick web in one of the corniches. As Boyd watched, the spider slowly lowered itself to the floor and scurried away.

Edina began to address the audience in her own language. She spoke for a few moments until she was interrupted by increasing applause from the back of the ballroom as Roma Lorta, flanked by bodyguards, police officers and Special Branch, finally made a rather melodramatic entrance.

Lorta was squarely built and very striking, with a mane of black hair that was swept back from his forehead. Boyd guessed he was in his early sixties and he certainly had charisma.

The applause became more sporadic, polite, far from ecstatic, but none of this seemed to faze Lorta. He strode towards the stage, flanked by his bodyguards, and the police and Special Branch officers fell back and began to position themselves around the perimeter of the ballroom. The scattered applause grew a little louder as Lorta reached the stage and leapt athletically up the steps while his bodyguards followed, spreading out in a semicircle behind him. He went immediately to the microphone, tapped it and began to speak in a seamless flow.

Unable to understand a word, Boyd found the atmosphere increasingly soporific, and he had to fight to keep himself alert. The ballroom was unheated, but the crush of bodies made the place stuffy and oppressive. Lorta's delivery seemed to go on indefinitely, without the slightest pause or hesitation, and again and again Boyd found himself drifting.

To keep himself awake, he decided to watch the audience. Some appeared openly hostile, others were much more supportive, but the majority clapped Lorta sporadically, maybe trying to make up their minds about him.

Boyd fiddled with the Seekers notice on his desk and once or twice took the luxury of closing his eyes. He felt deeply oppressed, as if Lorta's wall of words was thickening like a scarf around his neck. Through half-closed eyes he saw the main doors of the ballroom slowly open and a couple of latecomers arrive. They searched in vain for seats and ended up leaning against the wall, finding a small space between the police officers.

Lorta continued, his voice deep and expressive, occasionally using his hands in a gesture of embrace, as if he wanted those who were uncommitted to follow him, trust him, even love him.

Boyd's eyes began to close again and he was only dimly aware that the doors had opened for a second time.

Lorta was becoming increasingly intense and the crowd, at last seemingly moved by his words, began to listen more carefully.

Suddenly someone screamed, the sound so high and sharp that it was like a bark in the night. Boyd got to his feet and saw a slim young man walking towards the stage. He had a camera in his hand and moved in the direction of the press corps who were standing to the right of the stage. He seemed utterly focused, as if he was completely unaware of his surroundings, as if he only had one thought, one desire, one aim, one ambition.

He paused half-way to the platform, staring up at Lorta who, amazingly, was still speaking, impervious to the interruption.

Slowly the young man bent down and put his camera on the floor.

In seconds Boyd was on his feet.

'Stop him!' he shouted.

But the young man pulled an object out of his pocket and lobbed it on to the stage.

The grenade fell short, making impact somewhere in the audience. Then another figure stood up, this time near the front of the ballroom, and hurled his grenade towards the stage. The two explosions, one after the other, darkened the ballroom with smoke while Boyd watched bodies being blown apart, limbs scattering, carnage mounting.

Seemingly uninjured, Lorta was staring down at the smoke and the flying body parts in numbed disbelief.

At the back of the ballroom, Boyd could see Hilary Browning, also on her feet, staring ahead as if transfixed.

As a third grenade was lobbed at the stage, Boyd saw

Mile Kropitz and Josif Genzo in flames, beating at their clothes, trying to cover their faces with hands that were torn and bloodied. They began to stagger down the steps, the two of them suddenly becoming a human fireball, joining in the one great primeval scream of pain which was picked up by the panicky audience – a collective cry in the thickening smoke, with flames leaping to the ceiling.

Boyd saw a police officer lying in front of him. His legs had been blown off and below his waist was only a bloodied pulp. Just behind him lay a flaming corpse without a head. Then Boyd saw the missing head lying on the stage.

The smoke thickened again but Boyd was just able to make out Lorta running down the steps. Miraculously, he still seemed unharmed.

'Over here,' shouted Boyd with considerable authority, his voice penetrating the deadly confusion.

Then Lorta was at his side, mouthing words, face blackened and one of his hands bleeding from the wrist.

Now that Lorta had left the stage and plunged into the dense smoke, police officers and Special Branch didn't seem to be making any attempt to find him. One young man with a camera had undermined a whole security operation. The assassination attempt had been almost casually simple in its deadly chaos.

'This way.' Boyd was acting by instinct, grabbing Lorta's shoulders and propelling him towards an emergency exit. Pushing open the doors, they were pitched into chilly sunlight and a mass of passers-by, blundering through the melting snow and ice. 'This way,' yelled Boyd again, now conscious that he was not only uninjured but was actually leading Lorta to safety without the help of a single police officer, bodyguard or member of Special Branch. Both Lorta and Boyd were gasping for air, retching, trying to get the black filth out of their lungs.

Dimly he heard the roar of engines and looking across the road saw a couple of motorbikes speeding down the street. Boyd had a gut feeling he had just seen the assassins making their getaway.

Then he turned back to Lorta. 'I'll take you to a place of safety,' he shouted, wondering if he would understand him in the trauma. The grey streets seemed insubstantial, as if they were a cardboard set with paid extras giving the poorest performance, a gesture towards authenticity that was unconvincing and somehow unlikely.

Lorta had stopped choking. 'How can I trust you?' he gasped.

'I'm an undercover police officer. I don't have any identification papers on me. You'll *have* to trust that I'm taking you to a place of safety.'

They heard again the roaring of the motorbikes. Had the assassins seen them? Were they now hurtling back towards them, determined to finish the job?

'For Christ's sake, move!' yelled Boyd.

Lorta seemed to make up his mind. 'Where are we going?'

'To my place.'

'Where is it?'

'Not far.'

Lorta slowed down, slipping on the ice, nearly falling.

'What about my protection?'

'We've lost them,' shouted Boyd. 'Either you take this risk and trust me, or you're going to die.'

A bike came into view, the rider hunched over the handlebars, wearing no helmet, face exposed. He was somewhere in his early twenties, but Boyd had no idea as to his nationality. The bike weaved down the street, slowing down, the rider looking right and left. There was something shoved into the pocket of his leather jacket. Not a grenade, thought Boyd, but a weapon of some kind. He could be mistaken, but there was no time to find out.

'For God's sake,' Boyd yelled at Lorta. 'Follow me!' He darted down a side road and then looked back. To his relief he saw that Lorta was not only following him, but was actually catching him up. He was out of breath, but then so was Boyd. A stitch in his side was making him wince with pain, but he forced himself on, across another road and then another, wrenching open the glass doors to the block of flats, blundering into the hallway with its broken bicycle parts and scattered junk.

'One floor up,' he gasped, and together Boyd and Lorta raced up the stairs.

Boyd fumbled for his key, flung open the door and Lorta rushed in behind him, almost knocking him over, collapsing on the bed and then sitting up, his breath coming in short harsh gasps.

'I was a fool,' Lorta eventually managed.

'To come with me?'

'I should have waited for my security.' He fumbled out a mobile from his coat pocket and dialled a number, but there was no reply. He dialled again, with the same result.

'No response?' asked Boyd with what he later considered was stunning banality.

'I'll try another number.'

But there was still no reply and Lorta gazed down at the mobile as if it had a life of its own and was determined to frustrate him.

'What am I going to do?' he asked, looking at Boyd properly for the first time. Lorta seemed puzzled, as if he'd become detached from a world he had trusted.

'Stay here. Wait till things calm down,' Boyd advised him.

'You must have *some* identification?' Lorta pleaded.

'I'm sorry, I don't. It's too dangerous.'

In his sordid little room Boyd noticed that Lorta seemed to have completely lost his charisma. He didn't look as distinguished as he had thought him, and his hands were shaking, face grey and drawn, skin flaking, especially around the nose.

'I shouldn't be here,' he muttered.

'I can contact security.' Boyd brought out his own mobile.

'So can I,' said Lorta.

They looked at each other's mobiles as if they were playing Russian roulette.

'That was terrible. Fatalities must have been –'

'Impossible to tell,' Boyd interrupted, not wanting to commit himself.

There was the sound of sirens screaming outside and for a while there was silence inside the squalid room.

Boyd began to push the buttons on his mobile. Fortunately, Creighton replied.

'Two guys,' said Boyd. 'They got away on motorbikes after lobbing grenades. How the hell could they have got through security?'

'God knows.'

'We need to find out.'

'Yes, but Lorta's disappeared. Where the hell is he?'

'Here. With me. In my room. I had to take evasive action. One of the guys – one of the assassins – he was looking for him.'

'I'll have Lorta removed immediately.'

'That's just what his assassins have been trying to do. Did I ever mention I thought this visit shouldn't go ahead –'

'I'll get someone out there as soon as I can.'

Boyd had never heard Creighton so agitated before.

'How long? I can't show him any ID and he's feeling insecure.'

'I'll call you back.'

Lorta nodded as Boyd explained what Creighton had said.

'I'm grateful.' Lorta paused, looking less wary. 'Who are you?'

'I told you.'

'Working for?'

'The Metropolitan Police.'

'Does anyone know your identity?' Lorta was recovering, returning to his former decisive self.

'The local CID – and a couple of police informers who were murdered.'

'I read about the killings.'

'But you still came. Why?'

'I needed to speak to the community here – to all the communities. I have to try to explain what we're aiming to do – to give them some hope.'

'You're having a mixed reaction?'

'Many people don't trust me.'

'How do you account for that?'

'Isn't it obvious?'

'You're seen as a puppet.'

'I know that.'

'Is there more to it?' asked Boyd.

'I hope so. Tito held the former Yugoslavia together. I can do a similar job.'

'And you don't regard yourself as a UN puppet?'

'In some ways, yes. The strings are being pulled, but I can cut myself loose.'

'That could be difficult.'

'But possible. There's very little alternative.'

'You must have many enemies.'

'More than most men, but I get used to it. What about these murders? Do you have any idea who was responsible?'

'There could be a connection with the community of asylum seekers here, but of course that could equally well be a false trail.' Boyd spoke slowly, almost pompously, deep in shock. The bloodied body parts, the smell of death, the deadly smoke and flame were still with him, but Lorta seemed detached. Boyd wondered how much violence Lorta had seen and how impervious he was to it.

'How helpful have my people been?'

'Very. Particularly one of the community leaders – Edina Milstein. Do you know her?'

'Only by reputation. She sounds a formidable lady.'

'And one of your supporters.'

'I hope so.'

There was a knock at the door and Boyd froze. He went to a drawer and pulled out the silenced automatic he'd learnt never to sleep without.

'Who is it?' he asked through the door.

'Police.'

'Identification?'

'PC James Furbank. Number 14326.' The words were spoken with a quiet authority.

Boyd went to the door.

'Is he OK?' asked Lorta. 'Is he who he says he is?'

'I'm afraid not,' said Boyd as he suddenly pulled open the door and shot the young man in motorbike leathers in the chest.

He fell back, dropping an automatic, spitting blood. The surprise on his face was almost comical.

He hit the side of the corridor, making a dark smear on the wall as he slid down. The blood was pumping from his chest, pouring over his leathers and on to the floor. A small pool was gathering.

'He made an elementary mistake,' said Boyd. 'His registration was wrong.'

'You're very alert, Mr –'

'I'm called Rick James.'

'Mr James.' Lorta looked down at the figure on the floor. The bright red blood was still pumping out of the hole in the young man's chest. He was moving slightly.

Boyd punched the buttons on his mobile phone again, calling Creighton who was unobtainable.

'He's still alive,' said Lorta, crouching down beside the motorcyclist.

Boyd bent over the writhing figure. 'Who are you?' he asked, not wanting to know the answer.

The motorcyclist's eyes were cloudy and he muttered something that neither Boyd nor Lorta could make out.

'Who paid you?' persisted Boyd.

'I don't know.' Boyd realized with a shock that the young man spoke in perfect, unaccented English.

'Who paid you?'

The young man shook his head.

'An ambulance is coming. Who are you? Who employed you?' Boyd knew he wasn't going to get any information, but had to continue because of Lorta's presence.

The young man made a grunting sound, his eyes widened and then stayed open, staring up at the ceiling.

'He's dead,' said Lorta.

Boyd nodded.

'You should have shot him in the legs.' Lorta was reproving.

'I didn't have much choice.' But Boyd knew that Lorta was right. He called Creighton again, but there was no reply. Boyd then called the police.

Leaving the door ajar, Lorta went back into the flat and sat on the sofa. Boyd joined him, staring down at the carpet, numb and conscious of renewed failure.

'I understand,' said Lorta.

'Understand what?'

'You had to kill him. There wasn't any time.'

'I thought if I'd tried to shoot him in the legs he would have fired at me and then of course at you. He could have finished what he'd started in the Grand.' Boyd knew he was trying to explain his actions away, to defend himself, rather than giving a professional explanation. Yet Lorta was agreeing that he had had to do what he had had to do.

'Have you killed before?' asked Lorta.

'Yes.'

'So have I. It never gets any easier, even in an emergency.'

'I'm sure you're right,' said Boyd. In fact killing the young man had been incredibly easy, had even given him the satisfaction of outwitting and destroying. He felt very depressed. Then with a stab of worry he wondered about Edina. Was there a chance she had survived?

'Edina Milstein. Did she survive?'

'Yes.' Lorta was confident.

Boyd wondered why Lorta *was* so confident and felt there was also something different in his manner.

'Did you know her – before all this?'

'No.'

'Are you sure?'

'Of course I'm sure.' Lorta was rattled, probably still in shock, thought Boyd. And yet –

Boyd was about to press him again when half a dozen Special Branch officers pounded up the stairs. One of them was wearing a bloodstained overcoat.

'The name's Reynard,' he said, gazing down at the young boy. He showed Boyd his ID. 'Who's this?'

'An assassin,' said Boyd.

'Did you get anything from him?'

'No.'

'Who killed him?'

'I did. I've got Lorta here. I couldn't take any risks.'

'He doesn't look old enough to have a gun – let alone fire one.'

'He's more at home with grenades,' said Boyd. 'He must have been given some training.'

'You're sure he's the right guy?'

'Yes. How many died?' asked Boyd.

'Over a dozen. And more injured. Badly.'

'I'm surprised there weren't more,' said Boyd.

'We've got to take Mr Lorta away now.'

Lorta gripped Boyd's hand. Then he turned to the Special Branch officer in the bloodstained overcoat. 'This visit –' Lorta seemed suddenly confused. 'I let out a ravening Balkan dog.'

The Special Branch officer stared at him blankly for a minute and then turned to Boyd. 'Forensic are on their way,' he said. 'You won't be alone for long.'

'That's a shame,' said Boyd. 'I prefer my own company.'

*   *   *

Boyd locked the door and dialled Creighton's number again.

This time he replied and Boyd wished he'd given himself more time to think.

'I gather a dozen people died, and there are more badly injured.'

'What a cock-up,' said Creighton. 'Thank God Lorta survived. OK, I remember how you tried to stop this visit, Danny. You were right. We were misadvised.'

'There was a huge security presence.' Boyd didn't want the compliment. Admissions of failure from Creighton were not part of their relationship.

'There was a complacent security presence,' snapped Creighton. 'People here seem to underestimate one important fact.'

'Which is?'

'The asylum seekers may well have escaped feudal warfare, but in some cases they brought it over here with them.'

'One of the assassins followed us here.'

'So I gather. Pity you had to kill him.'

'I'll be more careful next time,' Boyd promised cynically. 'Who do you reckon's behind the assassination attempt?'

'I'm afraid I don't know. But whoever it was used very raw English assassins.'

'What does that mean?' asked Boyd.

'I think it means that whoever set up the assassination attempt didn't have much clout. They weren't professional.'

'Is that why I wasn't contacted?' asked Boyd bitterly.

'Possibly,' said Creighton.

'So, it was all a waste of time. The robbery, the –'

'It's no use to keep harping on that. What's done's done.' Creighton was brusque. 'We had to make an attempt to reach them. Unfortunately, the attempt misfired.'

'Are you still thinking of pulling me off the job?' Boyd was trying to calm down.

'Not now.'

'Then leave me alone to get on with it. I've still got useful contacts here.'

'You need to be very careful that you're not drawing too much attention to yourself,' Creighton warned him. 'Where's Lorta?'

'Gone to a safe house, I would imagine – with Special Branch.'

'What about this Edina woman? She's on the central council. I gather two of her colleagues were killed in the attack. Can't she give you some leads?'

'I'll talk to her.'

As Boyd put down the phone he realized Creighton had barely acknowledged his rescue and protection of Lorta. Bastard, he thought bitterly.

The Grand Hotel was surrounded by the emergency services. Twilight was deepening and the snow had really begun to melt, slush running down the gutters. Fire engines, paramedics with their ambulances, police vehicles and TV trucks were drawn up in the square and the whole area had been closed to the public.

'I'm sorry,' said a police officer to Boyd. 'You can't come in here.'

'I'm from Seekers.'

'That charity?' The police officer sounded contemptuous. 'You're still not coming in. We haven't got all the dead out yet.'

Then Boyd saw Edina Milstein sitting on the steps. She was alone and covered in blood, sobbing, her head in her hands, shoulders shaking.

'Edina.'

She didn't look up.

'Edina Milstein.'

'You must move on now, sir.'

'Edina,' Boyd called desperately.

Finally she looked up. Then she rose slowly to her feet and began to walk towards him.

'Aren't you waiting for an ambulance?' asked the police officer.

'No,' she said. 'The blood isn't mine.'

'You can't stay at the Grand,' said Boyd. 'Why don't you come back with me?'

'You know Mile and Josif are dead –'

'Is Fitim OK?'

'He's alive. But he went to the hospital to be checked over.'

'Shouldn't you do the same?'

'No. But I must get cleaned up.'

'You can do that at my place.'

She shook her head.

Carl Bennett had pushed his way through the crowd after showing the police officer his ID. He was in a considerable state of shock. 'Christ – what a filthy mess. I gather the assassins were British and tried to kill you all and Lorta. But Lorta got away. Is that true?'

'*Is* that true?' Edina asked as the police officer hurried away to prevent other unauthorized people getting past the tape.

'Yes,' said Boyd quietly. 'I took him back to my place.'

'You seem to be very keen on taking people back to your place,' Edina commented.

'It seemed safe.'

'Nowhere's safe,' said Bennett. 'You can't be that naive.'

'The point is that Lorta is alive and probably wouldn't be if I hadn't got him away.' Boyd was defensive.

'Do you want to give me an interview?' asked Carl.

'This is hardly the moment.' Boyd was contemptuous.

'I'm going to change,' said Edina abruptly. 'I'll meet you at the Seekers office in an hour.'

'You shouldn't be out on your own,' said Boyd.

'I need to be.'

182

As Edina hurried up the steps of the Grand, Bennett turned again to Boyd.

'They're saying you shot one of the assassins yourself. You seem to be a key figure in all this – so how about that interview?'

Boyd knew that, as Rick James, he had to co-operate with Bennett.

'What do you want to know?'

Bennett pulled out his audio recorder. 'I'm talking to Rick James who works for Seekers, a small charity whose staff have been decimated in the carnage at Seagate – a carnage that an increasing number of local residents are putting down to the asylum-seeker community.'

'That's not right,' said Boyd. 'The assassins at the Grand were British.' Well, the one I killed definitely was, he thought.

But Bennett didn't seem in the least fazed. 'Three people have already died in Seagate, all of them connected in one way or another with asylum. Now another twelve have been killed in a terrorist attack on the Grand Hotel where Roma Lorta, the exiled head of the Balkan state of Lubic, was speaking to an audience of asylum seekers. Mr James, is the situation likely to escalate?'

Boyd hardly knew how to reply. Then he said, 'All I can tell you is that Lorta survived the attack, although some members of the asylum seekers' central council here in Seagate were killed.'

'I gather *you* saved Lorta's life.'

'It was pure luck. I discovered him amongst the debris and took him back to my flat to recover.'

'But your flat was not a safe refuge, Mr James, was it? One of the assassins followed you home and attacked again. You killed him, I believe. Please tell me, Mr James, how come you own a gun?'

Boyd had already anticipated the question. 'Because I was afraid I might be the next victim. After all, my president and colleague had both been murdered within a day of each other.'

'So the precautions you took enabled you to save Lorta's life.'

'It was pure luck,' Boyd repeated.

'Or the act of a very brave man. But tell me, Mr James, *where* did you get that gun?'

'It had been in my family for a long time.'

'How's that?'

'My father was a military policeman. He retained the gun as a keepsake.'

'So you brought it with you to Seagate – the gun, I mean.'

'Not straight off.' He laughed. 'I wasn't anticipating trouble.'

'Where does your father live?'

'Putney.'

'Can you give me his address?'

'No chance. I'm not having him harried by the press.' In fact Boyd's father had died many years ago.

'I'm not intending to –'

'OK,' said Boyd firmly. 'That's it.'

Reluctantly, Bennett put away his recorder. 'I'm sorry you can't say any more.'

'I've said quite enough already.'

'Have the police spoken to you about the gun?'

'Yes.'

'And they're satisfied?'

'Of course. But if you don't believe me you can ask DI Faraday.'

'I'll do that,' said Bennett.

Boyd walked slowly back to the seafront and then on to the beach where King had been so fatally attacked. The night was windless and the deadly chill had gone. Tiny waves dragged gently at the pebbles, and behind him, from the cliffs, he could hear the slithering and continuous dripping of melting snow. Taking out his mobile, Boyd punched in Creighton's number.

'I had to give an interview to the press.'

'Christ –'

'There was no way I could get out of it.'

'How did you explain away the fact that you had a gun?' said Creighton as Boyd had known he would.

'I said it had belonged to my father who was a military policeman and kept it as a souvenir.'

'You might just get away with that,' said Creighton sourly. 'I assume the interview will go out?'

'Is there anything you can do?' asked Boyd, grabbing the opportunity.

'No,' said Creighton. 'It's all in the public interest so you may even emerge the hero of the hour.'

'Thanks.'

'We'll all be looking forward to the news.'

'Of course.'

'Where are you now?'

'Watching moonlight on waves.'

'That should be calming. You've had a lot of exposure, Boyd – always a bad move for an undercover officer.'

Boyd looked at his watch. 'I've got to meet Milstein.'

'Where are you taking her?'

'To my flat.'

'Isn't that dangerous?'

'For who?' asked Boyd. 'Or do you think I'm going to shoot myself in the foot?'

'I think you've already done that,' said Creighton. 'I'll brief Faraday about the gun. But it's not going to be watertight.'

As Boyd approached the Seekers office he could see Edina leaning over the rails and staring out at the dark sea. She was shivering in the cold wind and her mood was equally bitter. 'We had protection,' she said savagely. 'And those bastards walked straight through it. How does that happen?'

'They were lucky.'

'Who were they?'

'We don't know yet. But they weren't professionals. Maybe that's why they did so well. Professional criminals behave differently.'

'How differently?'

'They're not so reckless. Let's go back to my place. You can't spend the night on your own.'

'Don't you think your apartment is a little vulnerable?'

'They know I'm armed.'

'What about someone slipping through the net again?'

'They won't.'

Edina paused. 'You worry me.'

'Why?'

'It doesn't matter.' She turned away.

When they got back to the flat, Boyd locked the door. He went to the bedroom and was surprised to find she had followed him. He opened a bottle of whisky and they both sat down on the bed.

'I'm sorry the room's such a mess,' he said. 'And that you now know I keep a bottle in the bedside cupboard. I've been used to better things – like a cell.'

'Don't worry,' said Edina, downing her whisky at one gulp and holding out her glass for more.

'Are you likely to get drunk?' he asked.

'Not drunk. A little tipsy maybe. So much has gone wrong. God knows what life in Seagate is going to be like after what happened this afternoon.'

Checking his watch, Boyd saw that it was just after ten. He turned on the TV and caught the headlines. Mayhem in Seagate. What else?

The newscaster was speaking sonorously, in tones of national importance.

'In the wake of the tragedy at Seagate, the Home Office is to take a careful look at the number of asylum seekers in each town. Seagate certainly has its fair share.'

'So they're going to divide us up,' said Edina.

'Wait,' said Boyd. 'Wait until we can see what conclusions are being drawn.'

'And now,' said the newscaster, 'over to Norman Clement at Seagate.'

The camera moved in on Clement, who was wearing a heavy overcoat and standing just outside the police cordon at the Grand.

'This run-down hotel, inhabited by asylum seekers, has just been the subject of a major terrorist attack. It's an attack that has already been preceded by the murders of three prominent local citizens, although it's not clear if the incidents are connected.

'At 3.15 this afternoon two young men dressed in motorcycle leathers broke through tight security inside the ballroom of the Grand Hotel, where a large crowd of asylum seekers were listening to a speech by Roma Lorta, the exiled President of Lubic who is about to return to the region with the assistance of the UK and US governments.

'The intruders threw grenades, killing nineteen people – asylum seekers, police and security officers – and injuring dozens more.

'A fleet of ambulances has taken the injured to Seagate District Hospital where at least six of them are known to be in intensive care.

'Roma Lorta escaped injury and was taken back to London by Special Branch officers, while one of the assassins – whose identity has not yet been released – was shot dead in an apartment block a few streets away from the Grand Hotel. Police have not released any details of the shooting.

'This is –'

Boyd flicked the control and the television was silenced.

'Christ!' said Edina. 'I can't believe such a disaster ever occurred. What the hell was security *doing*?'

'Security isn't an exact science,' said Boyd. 'How about calling me Rick?'

'Is that your real name?'

'For God's sake,' said Boyd, trying to get a grip on

himself and wishing he had been more sparing with the whisky. 'We can't be having another conversation like this. I'm an ex-con who would like to forget he's an ex-con and be able to make a fresh start. That's all I am.'

'But you're a man who is very much in the right place at the right time.'

'You know what it was like in there. Lorta came my way. I had to help him.'

'You're very professional.'

'Meaning?'

'I don't know what side you're on.'

'It keeps coming back to that. Think about it. Does everyone have to take sides?'

'Most people do. The ones who are worth knowing anyway.' She laughed suddenly and the tension between them eased a little. 'Unfortunately my side is split into so many factions that its structure is highly complex.'

'Do you think I'm a police officer?' Boyd risked.

'Going undercover? No – I don't think that.'

Boyd prayed the relief wasn't showing.

'Then who do you assume I'm working for?'

'One of the factions.'

'Come on –'

'But why not?' She was insistent. 'You didn't have the slightest hesitation in shooting one of your own country-men to protect Lorta.'

'I happened to be around at an opportune moment, as you pointed out.'

'Don't give me that. You're here for a purpose, Mr James. The question is – whose purpose?'

'Are you accusing me of lying?' said Boyd, hoping he sounded convincingly outraged but suspecting he had only come across as ruining an ineffective cover.

'Your story's too good to be true.' She laughed angrily.

'Nevertheless it *is* true.'

'I find that hard to believe.'

'For God's sake –' Boyd got up from the bed. 'If you don't believe me, why don't you just go?'

'I don't choose to go,' she said, deliberately pouring herself another whisky.

'Why are you making these accusations then? I put my life at risk. I even had to shoot the bloody assassin. What I should be is a national hero, not your whipping boy.'

'Is that what you want?' She smiled provocatively but he refused to be drawn.

'Come on – the visit's over,' he said, going across and opening the door.

'I'm not leaving until you tell me.'

'Tell you what?'

'Who you are.'

'I've told you. Now please go.'

She got up from the bed and dumped the whisky bottle and her glass on the bedside table. 'Where I come from, you have to be very sure of who you're talking to. And if you're not sure, you don't talk.'

'I've given you my explanation.'

'I'm not satisfied. I'm sure you have another agenda.'

'Guesswork? Intuition?' he sneered.

'I can feel you think you've got nothing to lose.'

'I've a good deal to lose,' protested Boyd and then saw that he was further incriminating himself.

'Now you're beginning to tell me the truth.'

He grabbed her arm and tried to drag her out of the room. She resisted and Boyd was suddenly aware of how much he wanted her. Kicking the door shut he put his arms round her and they both fell on to the bed.

They were almost immediately interrupted by the ringing of Boyd's mobile. He got up and reached in his pocket for it.

'Will you give yourself away if you answer?' she said mockingly. Boyd didn't reply and she grabbed the phone out of his hand. 'Hello? Who is that?' She listened and then said, 'I'm Edina Milstein. Who did you say you wanted? Oh, yes – he's right here.' She handed Boyd his mobile. 'It's someone for you. He didn't give his name.'

'Who's that?' said Boyd shakily.

'It's Creighton. What's going on?'

'I'm talking to Edina Milstein – I can't speak right now.'

'Is that all you're doing?' Creighton rang off and left Boyd standing in the middle of the room in silence, Edina's hostility growing by the second.

She was as good as he had expected – rough and powerful. Sadly, Boyd disappointed himself in both these qualities and the climax he had anticipated didn't occur.

He lay back on the bed, sure of one thing at least. He didn't stand a chance as Rick James. The alias was doomed from the start. Stefan Kovac had broken him. He would call Creighton tonight with his resignation. But where would he go? Boyd knew he had to accept he *had* nowhere to go.

'I'm sorry,' said Boyd.

'It doesn't matter.' Edina sat up.

'I didn't want to let you down,' he muttered.

'In the circumstances it's not surprising.'

The silence lay between them like a lead weight.

Chapter Seventeen

The second time around, thought Boyd. At least it had worked between them the second time. The sex had been good and he felt more confident now. Mentally and physically revitalized, he walked through the early morning streets which were lit by tepid sunshine. It was no longer so cold and Boyd's head felt clearer as he began to mull over the attempted assassination and its deadly toll. Why had the security arrangements been so ineffective?

Boyd wondered if there had been a change of heart by the US and UK governments. Maybe Lorta's return to Lubic was not viewed so optimistically now, and knowledge of the government's diminished commitment to him could have weakened security. There was even the possibility that security had allowed the assassination attempt to occur. Set it up even. Wouldn't that mean Creighton would have been in the know? And the potential of a puppet politician and a puppet undercover agent might have been combined.

Then he dismissed the idea. Creighton had to be trusted.

Boyd had arrived at the station and decided to have a coffee.

The buffet was straight out of *Brief Encounter*, with steamed-up windows and a glass counter that held fairy cakes which looked as if they were cardboard replicas. Maybe they were.

Drinking his bitter coffee, Boyd considered the murders that had presaged the carnage at the Grand. Day, King and Hanley. What did they know? And who had known them collectively? Despite the dangers of another interview involving Rick James, Boyd needed to talk to Carl Bennett.

As he walked through the slush, his thoughts returned to Edina Milstein. We have a lot in common, he thought. We're both displaced. We're on our own. And even if she suspected him, what did that really matter? Weren't they recognizing each other as fellow survivors? She had no one, and neither did he. Could there be a partnership? More than a friendship? Or was he just fantasizing?

But he didn't stop thinking about her, couldn't stop thinking about her, remembering the foothills she had loved so much in Lubic. Why couldn't they walk there together? But slowly a greyness came into his mind, the same colour as the slush. The greyness of truth.

Carl Bennett's apartment was in one of Seagate's rather more striking buildings, a fifties block with clean white lines and balconies curving around its six floors. The overall impression was of an ocean liner just about to set sail.

Boyd trudged wearily up to the second floor and knocked on the door of number seven.

He was about to knock again when the door suddenly opened.

'What is it?' Bennett looked as if he was suffering from a massive hangover.

'I need to talk.'

'About last night?' He seemed less than eager. 'You've already given me a rather unsatisfactory interview.'

'Are you going to use the stuff?'

'Some of it.' Then Bennett suddenly seemed to relax. 'I need coffee,' he said. 'Do you want some?'

'No, thanks.'

'Or are you a tea drinker?'

'I don't want anything.'

'And how is the hero of the hour?'

'Are you going to invite me in or not?'

Carl Bennett stood back and Boyd walked into the living room, amazed at how bleak and untidy the place was. Papers were everywhere, mixed up with books and cups of cold coffee, and the heavily stained carpet was covered with dirty plates and magazines. There were no pictures on the matt white walls, which accentuated the air of desolation.

'I'm sorry about the mess. I know I live like a pig. When I get to London it'll be different.'

'Why should it?' asked Boyd baldly.

'There's something about Seagate that makes for inertia.'

'Have you got a job in London?'

Bennett ignored the question. 'Do you want to watch the news?' He indicated an enormous wide-screen TV set and Boyd saw that one wall was covered with high-tech gadgetry, from a DVD player to the latest in sound systems and computers.

'No,' said Boyd abruptly. 'I don't want to watch the news.'

Below them a police car sped by, siren wailing, swiftly followed by another.

'Do you want to see the papers then? *My* paper even?'

'No.'

'Nothing like keeping in touch.' Bennett looked at him more closely. 'You look shagged out.'

Boyd felt irritated. Seen in his messy home environment, Bennett just seemed a loser.

'You *are* shagged out. Sit down, if you can find a space.' Bennett pushed some magazines to the floor; one of them fell on to a plate containing a half-eaten burger. 'I'm a fast food junkie,' said Bennett, seeing Boyd's expression.

'How long have you been working for the *Observer*?' asked Boyd abruptly.

'A couple of years.'

'I don't suppose you're well paid?'

'Not particularly.'

'So you increase your income from other sources?'

'Look at this tip,' said Bennett flatly. 'Don't you think this flat reflects my lowly salary?'

'That equipment doesn't.' Suddenly Boyd was making a connection, but it was murky. 'So why don't you tell me what your other sources are?'

'Why are you so interested? You're a charity worker. Not an interrogator.'

'After what's been happening here, everyone should be on the alert. Particularly me, as an employee of Seekers, and you as a journalist and member of the Ice Breakers club,' Boyd added rather portentously.

'Are you saying my life is in danger?' asked Bennett. He shrugged and turned away, dismissing the idea. 'The club was an antidote to the Seagate inertia we were discussing. And I enjoyed their company.'

'They give you leads?'

'OK,' said Bennett abruptly, rather as if he had lost confidence. 'I'll come clean.' He held up his hands in mock humility. 'I've got an arrangement with the *Dispatch.*'

'The point is, have you got a job with them?'

'I'll be taking up a senior reporting post next week.'

'And you've been working as a – as a stringer?'

'Your media talk is a little dated, but – yes, that's roughly what I've been doing, and still am.'

'Do you think the attempted assassination was an inside job?'

'How do you define an inside job in this context?' asked Bennett, and Boyd could feel the tension rising between them.

'The asylum seekers themselves might have hired the assassins. Or alternatively, Lorta was set up by MI6.'

'How do you make that out?'

'It's just a possibility. Lorta was going to be a UN puppet. But maybe that's no longer necessary.'

'I don't understand the circumstances,' said Bennett.

194

'Neither do I,' replied Boyd.

'One thing though . . .'

'What's that?'

'Those young men. They weren't professionals. Wouldn't you agree?'

'Yes.'

'I would have thought MI6 would have used professionals.'

Boyd didn't reply and there was a long silence. Then Bennett said quickly, 'What do you want me to tell you?'

'I'm still trying to work out who was doing the hiring. Was it the asylum seekers, or maybe some fascist group? Did the government turn a blind eye? Was that the way it was done? Forget MI6 taking the initiative. They may not have needed to do that.'

Bennett was interested. 'You could have a point. Have you got any evidence? The *Dispatch* has offered me £25,000 for the inside story of the "terrorist attack" as they call it.' Bennett picked up a notebook from a desk in the corner that was covered in tea and coffee mugs as well as the remains of a sausage roll. 'Now it's my turn to ask you a few questions, Mr James. I'm afraid I can't answer yours, but you might be able to answer mine.'

Boyd was annoyed. He'd hoped to get Bennett's opinion and keep clear of a cross-examination, but he couldn't back off now.

'First of all, tell me why Edina Milstein was in your flat.'

'She was in shock and needed protection.'

'You're getting to be like an official for the Red Cross. Do you specialize in care and protection? Only a few hours earlier you'd been doing the same for Lorta. Presumably he was in shock too?'

'Very much so.'

'So you snare Lorta in your web, and then Milstein. Lucky break, was it?'

Boyd was suddenly certain that Bennett was on to him

and could blow his cover any moment. Why the hell hadn't he kept out of his way? Boyd could already see the discomforting headline: POLICE INSIDER SHELTERS ROMA LORTA.

Creighton would be furious.

But there was no way he could back out of the interview now. That would only confirm Bennett's suspicions. He had to think on his feet.

'Let's go back to the gun,' said Bennett. 'You're a charity worker – not a bodyguard.'

'I'm still a charity worker and want to stay one.'

'What does that mean?' asked Bennett.

'It means that before I joined Seekers I was what you might call a small-time villain. I know a dangerous situation when I see one.'

'So as soon as you'd taken a look at Seagate you thought you needed to arm yourself?' Bennett placed his notebook on the cluttered table between them and smiled hesitantly at Boyd.

Realizing they were both back to square one, Boyd returned his smile blandly, but inwardly he felt uneasy. Bennett's notebook seemed as deadly as any weapon.

'No.'

'Then what was the procedure?'

'When the killings started I was sure I needed to protect myself.'

'You'd hardly arrived.'

'I was worried that the people at the centre of all this might think I knew their identity. That Day and Hanley could have let something drop.'

'That's not necessarily why they were killed.'

'But the most likely explanation.'

'Have you used a gun before?'

'No.'

'You expect me to believe that?'

'I don't give a damn what you believe.'

'You will when another interview goes into print.'

Boyd shrugged.

196

'Someone said you were a born-again Christian, Mr James.'

'I was once.'

'What happened? Did you lose your faith?'

'It wasn't strong enough,' Boyd explained, knowing that in order to deflect Bennett he would have to flesh out Rick James.

'But it appealed to Seekers and got you the job.'

'It didn't appeal to Hanley,' said Boyd drily. 'He was an atheist. But he was satisfied that I was a small-time villain who wanted to make a fresh start. He'd have run a police check on me anyway.'

'He had a short cut for that. Did you know that Hanley was a police informer?'

There was a short silence while Boyd thought hard. 'No. I had no idea,' he said. 'How did you find out?'

'One of the asylum seekers told me,' Bennett replied easily, watching Boyd with some amusement.

'Who?'

'I'm afraid I can't give away my sources.'

Boyd decided to take a risk and push harder.

'You know there was another informer?'

'Yes?'

'Jack King.'

Bennett gazed across at him. He seemed to be making a calculation. Then he said, 'How did you know?' But he didn't give Boyd time to reply. 'Don't tell me. We're talking about Hanley, aren't we? Did Hanley tell you?'

Boyd nodded, pleased that Bennett had jumped to the wrong conclusion.

'All right, Mr James. Before yesterday's massacre, we thought we had a serial killer in Seagate – and maybe we did. Why do you think they were murdered?'

'For what they knew,' said Boyd promptly.

'But after that the trail goes cold?'

There was an uneasy silence.

Then Bennett asked, 'The guy you shot – had you ever seen him before?'

'No.'

'Have the police identified him?'

'How should I know?' replied Boyd blandly.

'One more question then,' said Bennett.

'What is it?'

'I could make it worthwhile for you to tell me about your real involvement.'

'How much?'

'Say five grand.'

'They must be paying you well. But no.'

'Ten.'

'I'd like to take the money and run.' Boyd was much more confident now. 'But there's just one catch.'

'Which is?'

'This is my real involvement. I'm a small-time crook turned charity worker. Ex-born-again Christian.'

'So why did you turn to Christianity in the first place?' asked Bennett in disappointment, clinging to the wreckage of the conversation.

But Boyd was feeling much more relaxed now – and he spoke with a fluency that he had never experienced before in Seagate. 'I've just spent six years inside. They were six very long years and we were three to a cell. The other guys were animals, but I can look after myself and they soon understood that. They spent their time wanking and telling me about the sexual conquests they'd already made – and those they were going to make once they got out. They brutalized me. Then I had a visitor.'

'Don't tell me – a born-again Christian.'

'No,' said Boyd with triumph, pleased to be keeping so professionally cool. At last he was behaving like an insider should – inventive and intuitive. Could he really be back to form? 'It was my partner. She came to tell me she'd met someone and was leaving me. I nearly cracked up – stuck in a cell with two fucking animals. I kept asking for a transfer and then one of them got parole. Someone else came to share the cell. It was a miracle.'

'The born-again Christian?' persisted Bennett.

'Yes. He was incredible.'

'In what way?'

'He was completely self-contained.'

'I don't understand.'

'He had terrific inner reserves. No one could get at him. He was his own man and his belief in God had given him resolution. I was completely convinced by the way he upheld his own moral standards, however difficult things were.'

'Do *you* match up to those standards, Mr James?'

'I'm working at them,' said Boyd.

Chapter Eighteen

As Boyd walked back along the promenade he thought over his dangerous discussion with Bennett. Had it been worth putting himself under scrutiny again? Bennett hadn't come up with any fresh information and although he had certainly given himself away in terms of ambition, what did that amount to? So the guy worked for a London paper. So he was making himself a lot of money. So what?

'Forty-forty,' came Arthur's all too familiar voice. 'Forty-forty.' The disturbed young man was holding his football as high as ever – but his arm was shaking. 'I'm going to hell,' he confided.

'See you there,' replied Boyd.

Leaning over the promenade railings, Boyd gazed down at the sea. There was still no wind and the water looked glassy, barely moving, even the tiny waves quelled.

On impulse, Boyd left the seafront and began to walk back into the town centre which seemed even bleaker in the mid-morning light, without the covering of snow, the grey slush melting in the tepid winter sunshine. The asylum seekers were now keeping to their box-like apartments, and instead the streets seethed with TV camera units, press photographers, reporters, producers, directors, all trying to push past the enormous police presence that had been set up outside the Grand.

The steps were covered in police tape and a large truck,

labelled INCIDENT ROOM, had been moved from the promenade near the beach where King had been killed, and set up on the opposite side of Audley Square.

Boyd watched for a while, his mind churning with information but not making any connections.

Returning to the deserted Seekers office at the head of the pier, he unlocked the door and decided to call Creighton.

When he got him after a long delay, Boyd asked if the identity of the young assassin had been discovered.

'His name was Raymond Wilson,' said Creighton. 'He lived in Broadstairs and was nineteen years old. He worked as a shelf filler in Tesco and was the only son of a widowed mother. He hadn't got a record and appeared to have been popular, much liked – but a bit of a nonentity. He sang in the church choir and helped out at a youth club. Interests were football and swimming.'

'This is the guy I shot?' Boyd was incredulous. 'He was pointing a gun at me. Just before that he'd been throwing grenades in a highly professional manner – along with his equally young companion.'

'There've been no reports of anyone missing amongst Wilson's friends and acquaintances; none of them fit the descriptions of Wilson's companion and no one so far has recognized his description. So we've drawn a blank at present. As to the people who hired him, we still haven't a clue. What have you come up with?'

'Not a lot,' Boyd admitted, and told Creighton about Bennett.

'We haven't been too clever about this,' Creighton admitted. 'We anticipated they would need professional criminals, or even *one* professional criminal. Instead of that they went for naive teenagers who wanted the ready money.' He paused and then added thoughtfully, 'Unless they're just scapegoats.'

'I saw them,' Boyd insisted. 'I saw them throw the grenades.'

201

'Did you get a really close look at them – in all that mayhem?'

'One of them came to my door and I shot him dead – remember?'

'That doesn't mean he was the assassin. It could have been a carefully planned deception.'

'He was armed,' said Boyd. 'He was going to kill me and get to Lorta.'

'And you had to shoot him. Don't start worrying about that.'

Boyd was surprised. Creighton was rarely encouraging.

'There's something else,' said Boyd.

'What?'

'If MI6 were involved, would you know?'

'Not necessarily. That's a depressing question.'

'It's a depressing world,' snapped Boyd. 'Hadn't you noticed?'

Boyd lay on the bed, watching TV, wondering what he should do next. If Rick James was to survive he had to deliver the goods.

Idly flicking from one news channel to another he eventually returned to CNN.

'And there are indications that the young man shot at 19 Telescope Mansions was connected with the assassination attempt on Roma Lorta at the Grand Hotel at Seagate where the death toll is rising. Twenty-one people, asylum seekers and police officers, have now died as a result of the incident.

'At the moment we still have no idea why the young man visited 19 Telescope Mansions or who was in the flat. No one has been identified as yet either by the police or the security services. Roma Lorta has now returned to London where he is resting after the attack and the resultant carnage. He has made no comment so far.

'However, DI Faraday, who is heading up the crime

scene investigations in Seagate, did speak to our reporter a few minutes ago.'

Faraday came on camera, looking flustered and tense. 'The outrage, with its resultant loss of life, is being carefully investigated. The attempt follows the murder of three prominent Seagate citizens – George Hanley, the manager of Seekers, the charity dedicated to helping asylum seekers in the town, Harry Day, local businessman and president of this same charity, and Major Jack King, another local businessman.

'Two of the three men were members of the Ice Breakers – an all-year-round sea swimming club – but so far this doesn't seem significant. All three had strong views about the asylum seekers – Day and Hanley for, and King against – and we are pursuing this as a line of enquiry.'

The camera then returned to the newscaster. 'Two of the principal members of the large asylum-seeker community in Seagate were killed as a result of grenades being thrown during the assassination attempt in the ballroom of the Grand Hotel. They are Mile Kropitz and Josif Genzo. We were able to speak to another community leader, Edina Milstein.'

Boyd saw her on the screen, standing outside the Grand, looking distinguished and full of authority.

'In addition to Mile Kropitz and Josif Genzo, eight more members of your community have been killed during the visit by Lorta. Do you have any idea why this attack occurred?' asked the reporter.

Edina was composed as she replied and Boyd felt a rush of longing for her, not a sexual longing but just the need to be with her.

'Many of our community, our very diverse community, do not wish to see Roma Lorta in a position of power as he is often seen as a puppet of the British and American governments. Therefore his recent tour has been subject to much criticism amongst asylum seekers, not only in Seagate but elsewhere.'

'But you had no idea that anything like this was going to happen?'

'No.' Edina Milstein stared steadily back at the camera.

'Not even when three prominent local men were murdered one after the other, as a prelude to the assassination attack?'

'We imagined that a serial killer had been at work . . .' Suddenly Edina seemed much less confident. Don't waver now, thought Boyd.

But her next words came as such a shock that they left him reeling.

'That was bad enough,' she said. 'But something else happened very recently that I feel was also a curious, and tragic, factor – a factor that the police don't choose to mention. Some days before the killings began, a little boy was run over by a van that belonged to raiders who stole a considerable sum of money from a security vehicle just outside a bank. I do feel that this deeply distressing incident may in some way be connected with the tragic events we have all been facing in Seagate.'

She paused and was about to speak again when the reporter interrupted her.

'Can you tell us why you feel this particular incident is connected to the events at the Grand?'

'A major assassination attempt – the preparations for a major assassination – needs financing. Perhaps the raid on the security vehicle had something to do with this.'

'To pay the assassins?'

'Why not?'

'The young man who was shot outside the door of a flat in Telescope Mansions was British. Do you feel there was British involvement with the assassination attempt?'

'Anything is possible,' replied Edina reflectively. 'The situation in Seagate has always felt hostile, although we are also aware that the asylum-seeker presence in the town has become a great burden to its inhabitants. But we have nowhere to go and we are still dependent on Seagate's goodwill – if there is any left. Finally I would like to express my deep regrets to the relatives of the police officers who died in the attack, as well as those who were injured.'

'Could the assassins have been asylum seekers?'

'No.'

'Do you think the assassins could have been professional hit men, paid to target Roma Lorta?'

'I think that's a possibility,' said Edina. 'And I'm sure outside forces are at work. Asylum seekers don't have enough money to hire gunmen. We don't even have enough money to eat.'

Boyd slept for a while and then woke again to the nightmare of the events in Seagate. Hanley, Day and King. Hanley, Day and King. Hanley, Day and King – the names beat a rhythm in his head.

Then he added the name of Roma Lorta.

Boyd sat up and tried to get a grip on himself. His head ached and he felt cold and shivery, but he knew what he had to do. He could no longer convince himself that his suspicions should be avoided.

He called the *Seagate Observer* and asked for Bennett, only to be told that he was in London and wouldn't be available until the next day.

Slowly, muzzily, Boyd realized an opportunity had been presented to him. He was sure that Bennett knew more than he had revealed. Carl Bennett was an ambitious man and now he had the *Dispatch* to satisfy. Boyd wondered if he was going to break a story – a story that he needed to know much more about.

Gradually Boyd saw that he had to take the risk – the enormous risk – of searching Bennett's flat. He had no idea what he was looking for, but to know Bennett much better than he did might be an advantage – an advantage that was worth following up.

As he walked the streets to Bennett's flat, Boyd began to

think about Edina again. In fact she was rarely out of his thoughts and he wondered if, in some impossibly old-fashioned, romantic way, he had fallen in love with her. He felt a yearning, not so much a sexual yearning, but a desire to be with her, to let her begin to heal him. They'd both had tragedies. They'd both grown lonely. Wasn't this the time to come together, to share their losses, to know that life had been empty but could be filled by mutual strength? In some naive daydream, Boyd imagined calling Creighton. 'I'm going to leave the force,' he told him, but all Creighton could reply was 'Let the force be with you.'

Boyd laughed aloud at his fantasy.

'Forty-forty,' said Arthur as he passed him, the arm holding the football trembling a little. 'Forty-forty.'

Boyd laughed again. He and Arthur could be quite an item if they got together, a couple of madmen on the tarnished streets of Seagate.

Boyd checked out the narrow alley that ran beside the flats where Bennett lived. To his relief he found that there was a fire escape to each rear entrance. The light was beginning to fade and Boyd was able to shift the lock with a strip of plastic without being observed.

The door opened without a sound and Boyd crept into the squalor of Bennett's untidy flat.

Stumbling over debris on the floor, Boyd looked down to see that he was standing on a plate that still contained a large helping of chips.

Dragging the torch out of his pocket, he cautiously switched it on.

Putting on his gloves, Boyd began to search, and half an hour later was still searching. His first discovery from correspondence in a bedroom drawer, lying under a layer of socks, was that Bennett was gay and had just finished an unhappy love affair. The relationship had concluded in a bitter exchange of letters that deeply, unexpectedly moved

Boyd. The rancour had all but obscured the former love the two men had had for each other but every now and then a hint broke through. 'When we made love in that hotel in the New Forest', 'When you took my hand in Stoke Newington', 'The time we had at Paul's barbecue', and so on.

Leaving the letters, Boyd began to concentrate on the small antique desk in the untidy living room and, listening intently for any sign of Bennett's return, he went through a number of shallow drawers and tiny cupboards, eventually arriving at the top of the desk which was locked.

Cursing, he searched the desk drawers again and eventually found a small key in a tiny wooden box. Inserting the key into the lock at the top of the desk he felt a surge of relief as it turned. Shining the torch inside he pulled out a pile of densely packed papers: share certificates, out-of-date press passes, Bennett's passport and his birth certificate, as well as the death certificate of his father. Then, when he'd almost given up, Boyd at last found something significant.

There was an advice note made out to Bennett for £8,000 and the lettering on the heading was written in Cyrillic, one of the Slavic alphabets.

Picking up the note, he looked round the living room, wondering if Bennett had a copier. After a long and nerve-racking search, Boyd eventually found one amongst the untidy jumble of equipment in a particularly cluttered part of the room. When he'd copied the advice note, Boyd put the original back in the top of the antique desk and locked it again.

For a while he switched off the torch and stood listening in the darkened room.

Then he went to the bedroom door that led back on to the fire escape. Closing the door behind him he clambered down. Pausing and checking to make sure there was no one about, Boyd walked casually up the alley and into the high street.

He went straight to the offices of the *Observer* and asked

the surly receptionist if he could see Bennett's editor, Colin Chambers.

'Name?' said the receptionist.

'Rick James,' snapped Boyd.

'Do you have an appointment?'

'Yes.' He glanced again at his watch. 'At 6 p.m.'

The receptionist fumbled in a desk diary. 'I don't have a record of that appointment,' she said triumphantly. 'This is the weekend, you know. We're not doing a late shift.'

'Well – I have it in my diary,' said Boyd impatiently, wondering if Chambers could be leaving the building by another door while this wretched girl played her petty power games.

She sighed.

'Is he in?'

'Yes.' She picked up the internal phone which was answered immediately. 'There's someone to see you – a Mr James.'

'I'm from Seekers,' Boyd rapped out.

'He's from Seekers, and says he has an appointment with you. No, there's nothing in the book. You'd like to see him?' She sounded both amazed and annoyed. 'I'll send him up.'

The receptionist gave Boyd a bright and artificial smile which seemed to say, 'You're here on sufferance. Give us as little trouble as you can.'

In fact she spoke like a disapproving automaton. 'Please take the lift to the second floor. Mr Chambers will meet you there.'

'Mr James?'

'From Seekers.'

'I'm sorry, I don't appear to have you in the diary. My mistake – or at least my secretary's.'

'I definitely made an appointment.'

'Of course.'

Colin Chambers looked more like a Harley Street doctor

than a local newspaper editor, with his immaculately cut pinstripe suit, old school tie and highly polished shoes. Chambers was bald and his wide handsome face had a high colour, but his eyes held a cautious intelligence.

Chambers took Boyd into an immaculate office with a modest, highly polished desk that had absolutely nothing on it – not even an in-tray.

'So what did you want to see me about?'

'I'd like to talk to you about Carl Bennett. I gather he's leaving.'

Chambers said nothing for a disconcertingly long time while he gazed down at his hands, liver spotted right up to the crisp white cuffs.

At last he said, 'Yes. I regret his departure very much. But I'm afraid it's inevitable.'

'How come?' asked Boyd, knowing what the answer would be.

'I'm very sympathetic to the plight of the asylum seekers, even more so since the atrocities at the Grand. I'd initially gone along with Bennett's championing of the cause, but eventually I had to stop his articles because the paper was losing circulation. In fact we were haemor-rhaging circulation.'

Chambers had been speaking with considerable delib-eration, then suddenly he became a little more relaxed.

'As a result our relationship's become rather strained, to say the least.'

'Has he told you about his future plans?'

'No.' Chambers paused. 'I didn't realize he had any.'

'Did you know he'd been offered a lot of money by the *Dispatch*?'

'No. But how do *you* know?' Chambers was immediately suspicious.

'He told me.'

'I wish he'd told *me*,' complained Chambers.

Judging his moment, Boyd pulled out the copy he had made of the advice note he had found in Bennett's flat and placed it on the desk in front of Chambers.

'What do you make of that?'

Chambers scrutinized the document carefully, his face inscrutable.

'To your knowledge, has Bennett done any work for a Balkan newspaper or news agency?'

'No – although I see now that doesn't necessarily mean he hasn't. But this advice note's dated last month and Bennett hasn't been over there for at least two years.'

'Does the payment surprise you?'

'It raises all sorts of questions. How did you get hold of this advice note?'

'It was in the desk at his flat,' said Boyd frankly and Chambers frowned.

'What were you doing there, Mr James?'

Boyd decided that if he was going to get Chambers's full co-operation he would have to come clean. 'My name isn't James. It's Boyd, and I'm an undercover police officer.'

Chambers looked up at him steadily. 'You entered Mr Bennett's flat? Without a search warrant?'

'I told you, I'm an undercover police officer, and I must insist that you keep this information to yourself.'

'Do you have documentation?'

'Hardly.'

'Then how am I to believe you?'

'I'll get you my boss.' Boyd reached for the phone, dialled Creighton's number and then passed the phone to Chambers.

It rang for a long while.

Then to Boyd's intense relief Creighton answered and Chambers asked for the necessary identification. Once satisfied he put down the phone.

'So you burgled Bennett's flat.'

'I searched it – and found this.'

'Yes.' Chambers gazed down at it as if the paper should magically reveal more information. Then with a sigh he put it back on the polished glaze of his desk. 'There could be any number of explanations.'

'How frequently did Bennett go to the former Yugoslavia?'

'I told you. To my knowledge he hasn't been there recently. He did some background research out there a couple of years ago.'

'Could this be a payment for permission to use copy he wrote for the press over here?'

'The rights weren't his to sell. The paper would have had to give permission.'

'How well do you know him?'

'He's always very easy to talk to, but I wouldn't say I really know him.'

'Do you socialize?'

'An occasional drink after work.'

'And then his articles began to lose the paper circulation?'

'At first I stuck with him. But when he began to attack our readers' attitudes to the asylum seekers I knew he had to go.'

'Did he accept that?'

Chambers sighed. 'He seemed to. But I realize now it was because he had a job to go to.'

'And that surprises you?'

'Yes, Mr Boyd. It does.'

Boyd phoned Creighton from a shelter on the promenade and told him about Bennett.

'He looks like a subject for Special Branch,' said Creighton. 'I'll get them to check him out. Where are you going now?'

'Edina Milstein's flat.'

'You're not going to screw her, are you?' asked Creighton with mild disapproval.

'I already have,' said Boyd.

Chapter Nineteen

'What now?' Edina looked as if she had been asleep and was irritated to have been woken. She seemed lifeless and exhausted.

'I shan't keep you long.'

She led him back inside and they sat in opposite chairs. 'I need sleep,' she said. 'What is it?'

'I think Day, King and Hanley were murdered because they'd discovered Bennett's connection with the Balkans.' Boyd produced the advice note which Edina inspected, staring down at the document without expression.

She passed the note back to him. 'How did you get it?' she asked suspiciously.

'I went to see Bennett in his flat. He had to go out half-way through, so he left me there alone for a while.'

'That was stupid of him.'

'It was convenient.'

'A born-again Christian, burgling a flat?'

'Old habits die hard.'

'I thought you were a reformed character.' She was half-smiling now.

'I suspected him.'

'There's no doubt that there's been a payment for work done by Mr Bennett. Though it doesn't specify what kind of work.'

'To help with an assassination?'

'Mr James – why are you playing detective?'

'I'm simply reacting to a discovery.'

'To a theft,' she said. 'Have you shown your research to the police?'

'Of course.'

'And what was their reaction?'

'They were interested.'

'You don't feel you're acting way beyond your call of duty?'

'Maybe you've forgotten I had to kill a man,' said Boyd. 'I can't just walk away from all this. Of course Bennett could have been doing some journalism out there – or more likely was being paid for information.'

'But you read more into it?' she scoffed.

'Bennett could have been paid to hire a hit man.'

'Oh really. You sound like someone out of an early John Buchan.'

'You read Buchan?' Boyd was very surprised indeed. 'In translation?'

'Of course. I'd hardly be able to tackle the original. But I like his work.' She looked at Boyd speculatively. 'As I've said before – keep on saying – I can't make you out, Mr James. You seem like a shadow on the thirty-nine steps.'

'I didn't know they actually existed.'

Edina didn't reply. The silence was tense, eventually broken by Boyd.

'Terrible things have happened here,' he said. 'We're all at risk and everyone's under suspicion.'

'But why Bennett? He's been here, championing our cause, for a least a couple of years. Does that make him involved in all this?'

'Pursuing a hunch – that's what I'm about,' said Boyd.

'I don't think that's what you're about,' said Edina quietly.

'As the only surviving member of Seekers, I have every reason to make my own enquiries,' Boyd said firmly.

Edina Milstein shrugged and yawned.

Boyd spent the rest of the evening going through the files

in the Seekers office. They were scrappily kept and it soon became clear that Hanley hadn't had his heart in this side of things – if he'd had his heart in anything at all. What *had* he known? Day was an unknown quantity, but what about Jack King? The only scrap of evidence he had found so far pointed to Bennett. But Edina and Chambers were right; the advice note didn't really prove anything.

After an exhaustive search, Boyd had to admit there was nothing of interest in the records of Seekers – simply scanty chapter after scanty chapter of relentless human suffering, of endless waiting and dwindling hope for people who were continuously being hounded by bureaucracy.

He was interrupted by a knock at the door and he froze, remembering he had left the gun in his flat.

The knock came again but Boyd didn't move. Then, with considerable effort, he walked slowly and quietly from the inner office to the outer – and wrenched open the door.

DI Faraday stood outside, looking vaguely apologetic. He had a large parcel under his arm.

Back in the inner office, Faraday unwrapped his parcel.

'Body armour,' he said briskly. 'You need it.'

'You think I'm on the hit list?'

'Very high up on the hit list. Wear it.'

'OK. Any developments?'

'No.'

'I didn't think so,' said Boyd. 'I keep in close touch with Creighton. In fact I'm hardly out of touch with him. Usually he lets me off the leash. But this time I seem to need the leash.'

'This is a difficult case,' said Faraday flatly. 'Do you think there could be more killings?'

Boyd shrugged. 'If I could see some kind of shape to all this, then I might be able to tell you. OK, the assassination attempt could stand alone. But if so that leaves the question of why three men were murdered. If any of them were being threatened, why didn't they go to the police? And after Day was murdered, why did Hanley and King behave so passively? Why did they wait to be picked off?'

'I don't know.' Faraday was gloomy. 'None of us are getting any nearer.'

Boyd was stung at the thought of sharing a failure with Faraday. He didn't want that.

'I have reason to believe that the journalist Carl Bennett is receiving money from the Balkans.'

'As a journalist?'

'Maybe.'

'What's the alternative?'

'That he was setting up the assassination attempt.'

'The killings too?'

'It's a possibility,' said Boyd.

'Seems unlikely,' said Faraday dismissively.

Boyd was sure he was being followed. Every instinct told him so, but no amount of discreet checking could establish who it was. As a result he decided to take the initiative.

Reaching the ruins of Dream World he scrambled over the gates and waited in the shadows of the wrecked swing-boats.

Nothing stirred and Boyd moved stealthily over to the coconut shy and checked the cavity where the arms had been hidden. As he had suspected, the space was empty.

He turned abruptly, gazing out into the darkness, watching for movement. Boyd was wearing his body armour and carrying the gun. Neither gave him much reassurance.

Then he heard the sound.

What the hell had it been?

A cough? A grunt? Something metallic?

He was sure that the sound had come from some distance. He looked out across the lake and thought he saw a shadowy movement near a gaunt ruin. Was someone going in or coming out? There was no further movement and Boyd became sure that the figure must have been going inside.

He walked slowly round the lake, keeping close to the undergrowth and then having to move without cover, gradually gaining the ramshackle building with the legend GHOST TRAIN dimly emblazoned on the dark wall. Boyd edged closer to the boarded-up entrance which had been partly torn down to reveal a rusty-looking set of open carriages.

He stood and listened but couldn't hear anything. For a moment he hesitated and then forced himself to go inside.

Using his torch, he moved cautiously, several times stumbling as the twists and turns of the switchback rails obstructed his path. His torch beam began to pick up dusty plastic cobwebs, a large section of real cobweb as well as several clusters of papier mâché ghouls, skeletons and witches. He then began to pass set pieces, including a witches' sabbath, a headless highwayman swinging on a plastic gibbet on a plastic heath, and a male vampire dressed in faded evening dress sucking at the throat of a young and nubile girl. Both were waxworks, but in the torchlight they seemed shockingly realistic.

Boyd moved on, his eyes on the curve of the rail, when suddenly he almost plunged into a pool of dark water that had trickled through a hole in the roof.

Trying to find a way of avoiding the water, Boyd swung his torch beam round, seeing that some of the carriages had been partly pushed off the rails, their rusty frames embedded in a monastery roof where a group of monks were eating a pie that looked suspiciously full of human remains. A bit over the top for the kiddies, thought Boyd, and then stiffened. He had definitely heard a movement behind him.

He swung round, reaching inside his trouser pocket for the gun, but it had caught in the lining and before he could get the weapon out he was hit in the chest by a silenced bullet.

Although the missile hit his body armour, the impact knocked Boyd off his feet and he fell backwards, cracking his head on the upturned carriages of the ghost train. Acutely aware that his pursuer must be about to fire again, Boyd struggled to his knees and received another bullet in the chest. Falling backwards again with a jarring wrench, Boyd faked injury.

Was he succeeding in fooling his assailant? he wondered frantically. Would they think he was dying? Or would they come and check? If they did he would have to get them first. But he was lying in an awkward position to pull out the gun that was still tightly wedged in his pocket.

He gave out a loud groan and rolled over on the floor in the darkness, wrenching the gun out at last.

Boyd waited.

The wait was interminable and his heart was pounding.

There was no indication that his assailant had a torch but he had dropped his own which was somewhere on the floor.

Still Boyd waited.

Still nothing happened.

Boyd slowly rose to his feet and stood there in silence, his ears straining. Eventually he heard cautious footsteps retreating and he started to follow, stumbling over his torch and wasting precious seconds as he bent and scooped it up. Moving as quickly as he could, trying hard not to make any noise, Boyd edged along in the direction he was sure his assailant had taken.

Moments later, Boyd arrived at a set of battered black doors, one of which was hanging off its hinges. This was where the ghost train had once hurtled out of its labyrinth. He savoured the word. Did his assailant have a warped sense of humour? Had he chosen to lure him into the maze of the ghost train ride as a metaphor for the tangled skein of the killings? Had his would-be assassin revelled in the joke? Somehow Boyd didn't think so.

He hesitated before the battered black doors, hoping they would be noiseless. But the doors squeaked horribly as he pushed through them out into the darkness of the derelict, vandalized amusement park.

No one seemed to be around, although he couldn't be sure. A night breeze had risen, destroying the stillness, rippling the surface of the lake, making a rustling sound in the arid trees, stirring the rubbish that drifted around what was left of Dream World, rattling at the rides, fluttering over the rifle range.

Keeping to the shadows, Boyd ran as fast as he could for the security gate and began to clamber over.

A couple of police officers were waiting for him below.

'OK,' said one of them. 'Get up against the wall, splay your arms and legs and do it now.'

His colleague checked Boyd's pockets and immediately found the gun.

'He's got a shooter.'

'Don't move.' The police officer wrenched Boyd's arms behind his back while his colleague took the gun gingerly and placed it in a cellophane packet that he had withdrawn from his pocket. 'Don't move,' repeated the officer.

'I'm not going to move,' Boyd assured him.

'We heard shots.'

'Yes. I was being shot at.'

'Who are you?'

'The name's Boyd. Daniel Boyd. I'm undercover.'

'Don't give me that.'

'Ring Faraday.'

The police officers exchanged glances and one of them began to punch out a series of numbers on his mobile.

The phone rang and was eventually answered.

'I've got a Mr Boyd here. Daniel Boyd. We heard shots in the amusement park and caught him climbing over the gate.' He paused. 'It's PC Wilmslow.' He paused again. Then he said, 'OK. I get you.' He replaced his mobile and went over to Boyd. 'You can get up.'

218

Boyd scrambled to his feet.

'Sorry. We had to check you out.'

'All in the line of duty,' Boyd replied testily. 'I'm sure you understand why I can't carry ID.'

'Of course.' They now seemed slightly embarrassed. 'What the hell was going on in there?'

'Someone was following me,' said Boyd. 'I went into the amusement park hoping I could confront him, and he shot at me twice, in the ghost train ride. Fortunate I was wearing body armour.'

'It's your lucky day, sir,' said PC Wilmslow.

Boyd returned to his down-at-heel flat and tried to cat-nap, but it was impossible to relax and he simply lay awake, listening to the drone of evening traffic and the steady dripping of melting ice.

Eventually he got up and called Creighton.

'I can't sleep,' he said.

'I'm not your GP.'

'So I thought I'd take a look at the bodies of those murdered men.'

'Why?'

'I'd like to check them out.'

'Surely you can get Faraday to let you see the pathologist's reports?'

'I'd rather take a look myself.'

'You'll be treading on toes.'

'Not if you make the authorization.'

Creighton sighed. 'You're beginning to spread your wings too far in Seagate. This isn't the way to stay undercover. You know that.'

'Things are moving too fast and getting completely out of hand. Who the hell can be behind all this?'

'That's what you're meant to be establishing, Danny,' said Creighton drily. 'It's no good asking me.'

'The massacre at the Grand was more like a terrorist

attack than just an attempt on Lorta's life. And then there's the three murders.'

'What's new?' said Creighton testily. 'Keep at it and keep your head down. You could blow this apart. Talk to Edina Milstein and stop bugging Faraday.'

But Boyd still decided to phone Faraday. He felt resentful at Creighton's attitude. He wanted doors opened.

'Faraday?'

'What do you want?'

'Information.'

'Such as?'

'Where are the three bodies?'

'Where else but at the morgue?'

'You've been through their clothes. What did they have in their pockets?'

'They'd been thoroughly cleaned out. Except for a scrap of paper on Hanley. And that could have been an oversight.'

'On his killer's part?'

'Yes.'

'What is it?' Boyd had expected Faraday to be uncooperative and sure enough he was. He had met up with this before. Undercover officers were usually the subject of jealousy. Boyd couldn't imagine why. He had often longed to return to a more humdrum job – until he remembered that the routine would give him time to think.

'It looks as if a lot of copy is missing.'

'Copy?'

'There are just a couple of words in Cyrillic script. Do you want a photostat? I'm afraid you can't have the original.'

'It would have been helpful if you'd told me about this before.'

'No one's asked me to give you any help,' muttered Faraday dourly.

'I admire your initiative.' Boyd was contemptuous.

'I'll meet you at the Seekers office at ten.'

* * *

220

It was just after 10 p.m. when Boyd unlocked the Seekers office and went inside, putting on the smallest of the desk lamps and waiting for Faraday who didn't arrive for another twenty minutes.

'Sorry,' he said as Boyd let him in.

'Any developments?'

'The body count hasn't gone up, if that's what you mean. But with all these foreign drop-outs around anything could happen.'

'Do I take it you don't like the asylum seekers?'

'Do you?'

'They're in an impossible situation.'

'I wish they'd go home.'

'You think that's the answer?'

Faraday looked uneasy. 'I'm sure some of them could go home.' He sounded aggrieved.

'Even Seagate's a haven after what they've been through.'

'I suppose so.' Faraday didn't want to argue. He pulled a plastic wallet out of his jacket pocket. Inside was a scrap of paper.

Boyd examined it.

'Well?' asked Faraday.

'It's some sort of Balkan script, but I don't know which.'

'Dozens of them, are there?'

'No.'

'They were better when Tito had them pinned down as Yugoslavia. I admired that bloke. But maybe Lorta's another Tito.' He sounded doubtful.

'I don't think so,' said Boyd, still examining the scrap of paper.

'I need some leads.' Faraday was getting agitated. 'The whole town's been turned into a soap opera. TV cameras everywhere – and the sodding reporters are leaning on me. Are you going to help me out?' Faraday suddenly seemed dependent on him. But his volte-face was of little use to Boyd.

*   *   *

221

Boyd knocked on Edina's door.

She took a long time answering.

'What do you want?'

'You,' said Boyd.

'I don't understand.'

'I want to go to bed with you.'

She gave a bark of laughter and Boyd smiled with satisfaction. He had never seen her discomforted before.

'Where have you been?'

'Trying to sleep.'

She shrugged and stepped back. 'You're like an animal,' she said.

'That's the way I feel,' replied Boyd.

'About me?'

'Yes.'

'That's not very flattering.'

'It's honest.' He moved towards her.

'Get out!'

'No.'

'I'll call the police.'

'I think you'll find them rather preoccupied.'

'Only because I'm an asylum seeker.' Edina's voice was bitter. 'The police here work on the basis that we're second-class citizens. Lower than second-class. They don't give a damn for any of us.'

'I'm not going to rape you.'

'How reassuring. Can't you get it into your head, Mr James, I don't want to have sex with you. Now please leave.'

'You want me as much as I want you.'

'I've told you to go.' But her voice lacked conviction.

'You don't want me to go.'

'You told me you were a born-again Christian, Mr James, or whatever your name is.' She gave a wry smile.

'I told you I'd changed my mind about that. But anyway, even born-again Christians have sex.'

'Not outside the family.' She was smiling and suddenly more relaxed.

'I don't have a family, so that presents a bit of a problem.'

'Yes – I can see that. I often feel the same.' She walked a couple of paces towards him and then paused. 'I just need to make a call.' She looked towards the phone that was on the living-room wall behind her.

'And I need to use the toilet,' said Boyd, knowing that he was in with a chance. But not much of a chance.

On his way to the bathroom Boyd had to go through Edina's bedroom. He could hear her talking on the phone and in her own language, but he knew he didn't have much time.

Boyd pulled open some drawers but found nothing significant. Then he began to check her dressing table which seemed to have come from the cheapest and nastiest of the self-assembly stores.

Boyd had no idea what he was looking for, nor could he imagine for one moment that he would find anything.

He pulled at the bottom drawer and then froze.

Why was she silent? Was Edina listening to the person she had called? Or was she even now padding quietly across the living room, ready to fling open the bedroom door and catch him snooping?

He froze, heart hammering. Why was he taking this crazy risk? Why didn't she speak?

Then she began to speak into the telephone again, making him start. She sounded angry.

He returned to his search, hands shaking.

After another couple of minutes, he opened a drawer to reveal a batch of photographs. Some were screwed up, cracked and torn. Others were untouched. Boyd picked up one of the more pristine prints and looked carefully at the rather shadowy image of a man. A middle-aged man who looked like a farmer. He was wearing overalls and his face was vaguely familiar. Maybe it was Edina's father. Hearing her hang up he quickly shoved the print into his wallet and hurried into the bathroom.

When he got back into the bedroom, Edina was standing naked, unselfconscious but vulnerable. Her body was firm yet slight and very pale, almost translucent, like a grey ghost.

Boyd paused, unable to take his eyes off her.

'Am I so ugly?'

'No.'

'Then what is it?'

'I'm sorry.'

'What *is* it?' she demanded.

'You just look great.'

'Don't give me shit.'

'I'm not.' Boyd walked towards her and put his arms round her waist. Then he lifted Edina Milstein on to the bed.

After they had had sex they lay on their backs, gasping. She had been vigorous and inventive and Boyd had enjoyed her immensely.

Then he turned to Edina and they did it all over again.

When they had finished, he said, 'It was so good.'

'For me as well.'

'Do you have anybody?'

'No,' she said baldly, her face sombre now.

'What about back home?'

She shook her head. 'I told you my life story. I can never go back. It's all finished out there for me now.'

'Bad things have happened here.'

'You mean I've been caught between massacres?' she asked with a shiver. 'You're right.'

'We could – make something of our lives.'

'Us two?'

'Why not? Or don't you –'

'I like you, Rick James, or whatever else you are called.'

'You're determined to find me confusing.'

She leant over and gently bit the lobe of his ear.

'I find you complicated. But I like complicated men.'

'Like Lorta?'

'I wouldn't say he was complicated,' said Edina.

They were silent. Boyd closed his eyes. Suddenly he felt exhausted. 'Can I stay here tonight?'

'The bed is not just for sex. It's for sleeping in too.'

Boyd sensed that he had upset her in some way and wondered why. Then he didn't want to look for a reason. He just wanted to sleep.

Edina leaned over again, but this time she pressed his eyes tight shut. It was a curious sensation. Her fingers were strong and the pressure on his lids hurt.

'You haven't offended me. Unless you were thinking of me as a whore.'

'I wasn't.'

Slowly sleep began to overwhelm him and he relaxed for the first time in days.

'Is there a chance?' he muttered.

'I don't think so.'

'You want to stay alone?'

'For a while. For a long while. Now sleep.'

The pain was blunt and numbing and for a moment Boyd thought he had pulled a muscle. Then, as he opened his eyes, he realized the pain was too great for that.

Still half-asleep he reached out and something incredibly sharp slit one of his fingers.

Boyd bellowed in pain.

Focusing at last he saw Edina's face and for a second, in his bewilderment, Boyd was reassured.

Then he saw she had a knife in her hand.

'For God's sake,' Boyd gasped as the pain rose. 'What the fuck do you think you're doing?'

She was standing beside the bed, staring down at the duvet which was fast becoming a sea of blood. His blood.

'I know who you are,' she said. 'You're not Rick James. You're a policeman – working undercover.'

How had she found out? he wondered as the pain receded slightly. Fleetingly he felt detached from his own body, as if he was looking down on the scene, dispassionately noting what was happening.

She lashed out with the knife and caught him on the shoulder, but as her arm came down again instinct took over and he grabbed at her wrist, pulling Edina across him and struggling for possession of the knife.

Now the pain was back and he howled in agony while she fought against him. Boyd kicked the duvet away and they rolled over, eventually sliding off the bed on to the floor.

Several times Edina almost managed to stab him again, but he was too strong for her, eventually managing to wrest the knife out of her hand and throw it into the corner of the room.

Then with a twist he was on top of her, blood covering them both, blood that was still pumping out of his stomach and shoulder.

The pain came back, this time excruciating, and Boyd screamed again and again. But somehow he drew on some inner strength and straddled Edina, grabbing her arm and twisting it until she was screaming as loudly as he was.

Looking down at his stomach Boyd saw the blood still welling up. How much had he lost? he wondered.

'For God's sake!' he shouted at her again. 'Why?'

But she made no attempt to answer him, still screaming, her voice high and shrill, matching his own howling, turning it into a joint cacophony, a primeval cry.

'Why?' he asked again, bellowing into her bloodied face. '*Why*? Tell me or I'll fucking tear you apart!'

'Kill me,' she hissed at him. 'Go ahead and kill me.' Instinctively Boyd put his hands around her neck and squeezed. He went on squeezing as she choked. Then he stopped. As he did so, Boyd suddenly made a connection.

Chapter Twenty

Boyd staggered to his feet, sick and dizzy, the pain increasing. He was still bleeding.

Edina was lying on the floor and he bent over her, wondering if he had killed her. Catching sight of the knife he picked it up and stumbled across to the phone. Never had he needed so desperately to hear Creighton's voice.

'Creighton?' he whispered.

'I'm here, Danny.'

'I'm hurt. I'm badly hurt. Edina Milstein – she attacked me.' Boyd began to gasp as the pain intensified yet again.

'I'll call for help. Where are you?'

'In her flat.'

'How bad is it?'

'Stabbed. I can't stop the blood. Stomach.'

'Wrap a towel round the wound. Where's Milstein?'

'On the floor.'

'Unconscious?'

'For the moment.'

'Get off the line.'

Boyd hung up. The weakness was filling him and now his vision kept coming and going.

As he turned away from the phone he saw that Edina had regained consciousness and was kneeling by the bed, covered in his blood. He remembered how she had sat outside the Grand, soaked again in blood. But never her own.

Boyd gazed down at the gash in his stomach from where his own blood was still streaming. How much had he lost? he wondered again. How much blood could he go on losing?

'That was for Stefan,' Edina said quietly.

Dizziness was overcoming him now but the pain had gone, and Boyd knew this was a very bad sign.

Edina stumbled past him while he slumped against the wall, longing to get on the bed, to find some comfort. He shouldn't have let her go, Boyd knew that, but the steady pumping of his blood and the red, congealing lake on the floor around him had undermined his judgement completely. His whole instinct was focused on the need to remain conscious, to cling to a life that he had often dismissed as worthless. What he had done to his family, and to Stefan, as well as the way he had so grossly mishandled this case, were now side issues. Boyd wanted to live, with all the primitive zeal of a dying animal. He *had* to live. There was so much to do.

Using his last ounce of strength he struggled to his feet, waiting for his attacker.

Edina returned with a large, thick towel, coming across to him purposefully, and Boyd gripped the knife tighter.

'I can't help you with that in your hand,' she said.

'You'll have to.'

'Let me help you,' she entreated.

'Why did you do this to me?'

'You're losing too much blood to ask questions.'

Suddenly Boyd threw the knife back into a corner of the room and held up his hands in submission, raising them above his head as she wound the towel tightly round his stomach.

'Stay where you are,' she said.

The binding of the towel around his wound made Boyd give a howl of pain. 'For Christ's sake!'

'Lie down flat.'

Boyd lay on the bed, the pain unbearable, whimpering and howling as she plugged the towel into the hole in his stomach. He knew he had thrown the knife away for a second time. She could so easily retrieve it. Yet, in a strange, instinctive way, he didn't expect her to do so.

'Your shoulder's a small problem,' Edina was saying. 'Your stomach is a very big problem.'

Boyd screamed again and again and she took his clammy hands and held them tightly. Her grip was the last thing he felt as he lapsed at last into unconsciousness.

Sometimes he woke sweating in the hospital bed, sometimes he woke screaming. Often he did both. At first he had injections for the pain; after a while they managed to get him to swallow tablets – but nothing seemed to stop the agony.

After a few days, Boyd developed a fever and lost contact with reality, permanently tramping the snow-bound, icicle-hung, freezing cold streets of Seagate.

Again and again he felt the bump as he ran the van over Stefan's body. Then he was standing on the beach, holding the dead boy's hand, gazing out at the winter sea. But when he turned to say something to Stefan, Boyd could see his eyes were wide open, staring sightlessly ahead.

'You'll make it, Danny,' said Creighton from a long way off. 'You've done it before and now you can do it again.'

Sometimes Boyd saw himself running down the steps of the Grand Hotel, miraculously restored to its former elegance, while the grim reaper with scythe followed him down the sweeping grandeur of the staircase. Then he was lying in a snowdrift by the side of the road, Stefan's flowers covering him like a blanket.

'Forty-forty,' said a voice in his ear. 'Forty-forty.'

Occasionally he surfaced.

Creighton was always there.

'I need to talk to you, Danny. I want you to fight back as

hard as you can. I'm relying on you, Danny. We need to talk.'

But Boyd was submerged, up to his neck in pebbles as the tide came in, icicles clinking in the surf which splashed over his face, almost suffocating him.

'I'm trapped,' he told Creighton. 'I'm trapped by the tide. It's a hot tide.'

Creighton took his hand in as strong a grip as Edina's. 'Fight.'

'I'm drowning.'

'Fight harder. You've done it before, and you can do it again.' The words were like a mantra.

Dimly Boyd remembered his car, spinning out of control on the motorway, the vehicle that contained the family he had destroyed all those years ago. The unbearable loss was still unbearable; the loss that had made him go undercover, exchanging one alias after another, living the lives of invented men.

'Stop!' he howled.

'What is it?' asked Creighton.

The nurse came and gave him an injection and then Creighton became more pressing.

'I need to talk to you, Boyd. I need to talk to you, Daniel.'

As if shouting from a very long distance, Boyd asked him what he wanted to talk about.

'Who is she?' asked Creighton. 'Who is Edina?'

'She tried to kill me. Where is she?'

'Under arrest.'

'On what charge?'

'Attempted murder. How much more can you tell me about her?'

'It's in my wallet.'

'What is?'

'The photograph. Get the wallet. Get it quickly. The pain will be –'

But Creighton was already at the cupboard by his bedside, checking through his personal effects, just as he himself had done in Bennett's flat and in Edina's apartment. When Creighton found the photograph he put it on the bedcover. 'That's Lorta,' he said.

'No it's not. It's Kerno.'

'Who the hell is he?'

'Lorta's brother. He shot Edina's mother. Lorta must have taken a fancy name when he moved up in the world.' Boyd's voice began to blur as the pain returned. He closed his eyes and saw Edina walking towards him, holding the towel, ready to staunch his wound.

Some hours later, when Boyd had surfaced again, Creighton was waiting patiently by the bed.

'She set up the assassination attempt?'

'It can't have been easy,' said Boyd.

'But her motive was revenge?'

Boyd nodded. 'What about Bennett?'

'He's also been arrested – and confessed. Maybe he'll be able to sell his story.'

'That sounds like him,' said Boyd. 'He killed the three men. They were all beginning to have suspicions.'

Later, on one of his better days, Boyd suddenly began to focus. The pain was still there, but he felt more coherent.

'You're going to live, Danny.'

'What for?' he asked.

'For me. To fill me in on everything you know. This is important.'

But he couldn't. The pain was still too great and Boyd felt swallowed up, inside the pain. He began to have a recurring dream of blundering about in the abandoned ghost train ride, unable to get out.

Then, amazingly, Boyd woke to more distanced pain, feeling as if he was standing on the pebbles of the beach at

Seagate, watching the tide slowly recede, leaving rock-pools and stretches of virgin sand.

'Did you ever suspect her?' asked Creighton gently, and his voice sounded as if it too was coming from a distant shore.

'Towards the end.'

'Did you suspect Bennett?'

'I wasn't so sure. But I think he was being paid by an intelligence agency in Lubic who didn't want Lorta to return.'

'So he was involved in planning the assassination attempt too?'

'Yes – they managed to botch it through together – and still get round security.'

'It was the amateur approach,' said Creighton. 'Not at all what security were looking for.'

But Boyd had lapsed back into unconsciousness, silently stealing over the snow-bound streets of Seagate, walking gingerly, conscious of the ice beneath his feet.

Later, he surfaced again to find the relentless figure of Creighton by his bedside.

'Why did Bennett kill the three of them?' he asked.

Boyd was silent. Then he slowly said, 'I've already told you.'

'I'd like to hear your conclusion again.'

'They were on to him,' said Boyd. 'He was recruiting – not amongst the asylum seekers, but amongst the gay rough trade. Looking for assassins.'

'That's why we set up the bank heist,' said Creighton.

'We were too late – and anyway, neither Milstein nor Bennett were looking for professionals. Just two young candidates, hand-picked for training.'

There was a long silence. Boyd was exhausted again.

Then he whispered, 'He only wanted money – Edina wanted revenge. Is that what she told you?'

Creighton nodded. 'That's exactly what she told me.'

'How long since we last spoke?' asked Boyd.
'A day.'
'So you do actually go home?'
'No. I've been sleeping in the hospital.'
'Good God.'
'You're valuable to us, Danny.'
'For this job alone?'
'No.'
'I appreciate your concern –'
'Don't go sour on me, Danny. Tell me more about Milstein. Did you suspect her as much as Bennett?'
'No. I didn't suspect her for a long time.'
'Didn't you get too close? So close you couldn't see?'
Boyd was silent.
'What will you be doing when you leave here?' asked Creighton.
'Recovering.'
'At home?'
'I'd never recover there.'
'How about San Diego?'
'That would be easier. Are you giving me a present?'
'I never give presents,' said Creighton. 'It's the rule of a lifetime.' He drew out his wallet. 'Here's your ticket – and the hotel is booked. It's expensive. Very expensive.'
'What are you offering me? Some kind of ex gratia payment?'
'Certainly not.'
'Then who is?'
'Roma Lorta.'
'Isn't that bribery?'
'I don't think so,' smiled Creighton. 'Besides, there's something I want you to do.'
'In San Diego?'
'Yes. You know the Dedalus threat? The child?'
'I've read about it.'

234

'You infiltrate,' said Creighton. 'While you're recovering.'

'With a wound this size?'

'That you got from a gangster chum who's also in the abduction business.' Creighton cleared his throat and stood up. 'Look – where do you want to be? Sutton and your home of painful memories, or San Diego in the sun – with a new identity?'

'I'll be a sick man.'

'That won't stop you. I know how much you enjoy new identities – and this one ensures luxury hotels and a substantial expense account.'

'What can I say?' asked Boyd.

'You'll say nothing,' replied Creighton. 'You never grew into Rick James. But now you have to grow into Lennie Jukes. And if you don't –'

'I will,' said Boyd. 'I'll put on another skin for you. Any time.'

When Boyd had recovered enough to walk, he decided that for his first halting exercise he should take a train from the London clinic to Seagate. When he arrived he walked down to the sea and watched the waves crashing on the shingle. There was a strong wind and the March day was full of buffeting gusts that were strong enough to strew pebbles on the promenade.

The grey-green shelters were full and as Boyd hurried past he could see the asylum seekers were still stranded in this faded outpost of Britain.

There was a long queue for the telephone box by the pier and he saw them patiently waiting, telephone cards clutched in hands, soon to speak to relations and friends in Albania or Kosovo or Bosnia or Afghanistan. Or Lubic.

Boyd strolled back to Audley Square and stood outside the Grand to find the hotel's doors had been boarded up, while a sign advised tenants to use the back entrance.

He looked up at the windows to see the same faded

curtains and newspapers hiding cracks in the glass – or the space where there was no glass at all.

Boyd turned away and summoned up the courage to walk across the square to the place where Stefan had died. The flowers had gone and there was no sign of their presence – not even a leaf. He glanced down at his watch. It was ten past three. Soon the schoolchildren would be out, some of them heading for the rooms of their parents in the Grand.

Boyd decided to wait and sat down on a bench. He gazed up at the windows of the Grand, trying to work out which window had been Edina Milstein's. But he seemed to have forgotten. He dozed off and then woke abruptly to see the groups of schoolchildren walking across the square, some of them hand-in-hand.

Again he looked up at the windows of the Grand. One of them had been opened, despite the blustering wind.

With a shock Boyd saw Rila Kovac's face. She was waiting and watching just as he was. But she was watching the children. Some of the boys had dark hair, long dark hair they were pushing out of their eyes as they ran across the square.

He longed to talk to Rila, to confess what he had done. Instead Boyd got up and began to walk slowly and regretfully back to the station.

236

MOBILE SERVICES
01633 256550

18/11/03 E